Wed in ...
Do You Take Th... ...rella
A Conard County Baby by Rachel Lee
A Randall Hero by Judy Christenberry
The Texas Wildcatter's Baby by Cathy Gillen Thacker
The Bull Rider's Son by Cathy McDavid

SHIPMENT 2

The Cowboy's Valentine by Donna Alward
Most Eligible Sheriff by Cathy McDavid
The Lawman Lassoes a Family by Rachel Lee
A Weaver Baby by Allison Leigh
The Last Single Maverick by Christine Rimmer
A Montana Cowboy by Rebecca Winters

SHIPMENT 3

Trust a Cowboy by Judy Christenberry
Million-Dollar Maverick by Christine Rimmer
Sarah and the Sheriff by Allison Leigh
The Cowboy's Homecoming by Donna Alward
A Husband in Wyoming by Lynnette Kent
The Comeback Cowboy by Cathy McDavid
The Rancher Who Took Her In by Teresa Southwick

SHIPMENT 4

A Cowboy's Promise by Marin Thomas
The New Cowboy by Rebecca Winters
Aiming for the Cowboy by Mary Leo
Daddy Wore Spurs by Stella Bagwell
Her Cowboy Dilemma by C.J. Carmichael
The Accidental Sheriff by Cathy McDavid

SHIPMENT 5

Bet on a Cowboy by Julie Benson
A Second Chance at Crimson Ranch by Michelle Major
The Wyoming Cowboy by Rebecca Winters
Maverick for Hire by Leanne Banks
The Cowboy's Second Chance by Christyne Butler
Waiting for Baby by Cathy McDavid

SHIPMENT 6

Colorado Cowboy by C.C. Coburn
Her Favorite Cowboy by Mary Leo
A Match Made in Montana by Joanna Sims
Ranger Daddy by Rebecca Winters
The Baby Truth by Stella Bagwell
The Last-Chance Maverick by Christyne Butler

SHIPMENT 7

The Sheriff and the Baby by C.C. Coburn
Claiming the Rancher's Heart by Cindy Kirk
More Than a Cowboy by Cathy McDavid
The Bachelor Ranger by Rebecca Winters
The Cowboy's Return by Susan Crosby
The Cowboy's Lady by Nicole Foster

SHIPMENT 8

Promise from a Cowboy by C.J. Carmichael
A Family, At Last by Susan Crosby
Romancing the Cowboy by Judy Duarte
From City Girl to Rancher's Wife by Ami Weaver
Her Holiday Rancher by Cathy McDavid
An Officer and a Maverick by Teresa Southwick
The Cowboy and the CEO by Christine Wenger

THE COMEBACK COWBOY

NEW YORK TIMES BESTSELLING AUTHOR

CATHY McDAVID

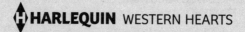

Recycling programs
for this product may
not exist in your area.

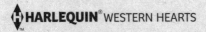

HARLEQUIN® WESTERN HEARTS

ISBN-13: 978-1-335-50775-4

The Comeback Cowboy
First published in 2011.
This edition published in 2020.
Copyright © 2011 by Cathy McDavid

For questions and comments about the quality of this book,
please contact us at CustomerService@Harlequin.com.

Harlequin Enterprises ULC
22 Adelaide St. West, 40th Floor
Toronto, Ontario M5H 4E3, Canada
www.Harlequin.com

Printed in U.S.A.

Since 2006, *New York Times* bestselling author **Cathy McDavid** has been happily penning contemporary Westerns for Harlequin. Every day, she gets to write about handsome cowboys riding the range or busting a bronc. It's a tough job, but she's willing to make the sacrifice. Cathy shares her Arizona home with her own real-life sweetheart and a trio of odd pets. Her grown twins have left to embark on lives of their own, and she couldn't be prouder of their accomplishments.

To Libby and Connie.
I always knew you would make great critique partners. What I didn't know was how much your friendship would enrich my life. Thank you for making the last ten years not just a journey but an adventure. I love you both.

Chapter 1

Welcome to Seven Cedars Ranch, Home of Cowboy College.

He sat immobile, staring at the large sign with its horse-head logo, his jaw tightly clenched.

Up until the moment he drove through the main gate, he'd been able to deny how really low he'd sunk in the last six months and how really far he'd have to climb to get back on top.

No more. The time to man up had officially arrived.

He reached for the door handle on his pickup—only to have it abruptly wrenched open. Startled, he turned to look into the face of a kid no older than eighteen or nineteen.

"Welcome, Mr. Boudeau. We've been expecting you." The kid waited, a gosh-I-can't-believe-it's-you grin plastered across his freckled face.

"The name's Ty." He removed the keys from the ignition and climbed out.

"A real pleasure to meet you, Ty." They shook hands. "Folks 'round here call me Stick." The kid stepped back, and Ty could immediately see how he'd earned the nickname. Stick could get lost standing behind a flagpole. "Right this way. Adele's waiting for you."

Ty hesitated, the doubts he'd successfully kept at bay during the four-hour drive across Wyoming gaining ground. He needed help, that was a fact. But from a woman? One who made a living instructing amateurs at a glorified dude ranch. For a professional tie-down and team roper like himself, the idea was ludicrous. Certainly not "genius," as his younger sister had professed.

And yet he'd come.

"Okay to leave the truck parked here?" His Ford F350 dually and horse trailer blocked all six of the available spaces in front of the rustic two-story lodge.

"No problem."

Being a minor celebrity, even an undeserving one, had its privileges, he supposed.

Grabbing his wallet, Ty followed Stick up a stone-lined walkway, across a sprawling porch and through the front entrance of the lodge. With each thunk of his boots on the hardwood floor, his gut clenched tighter. This place was his last-ditch effort. If it, and Adele Donnelly, couldn't figure out what he was doing wrong, then he might as well kiss his roping career goodbye.

"Here's the main lobby and that way is the business center," Stick informed him as they crossed the spacious room with its vaulted ceilings and pine beams. Ten-foot-high windows looked out onto rolling green grounds dotted with thick stands of trees. "The front desk is where you check in and out, get the weekly schedules, sign up for classes." He shot Ty a guilty look over his shoulder. "Not that you need any."

"You never know." He definitely needed something.

"There's a lounge with a TV over there for guests." Stick pointed. "It's got satellite."

"Oh, good. Can't miss my daily dose of CNN."

His attempt at sarcasm went right over Stick's head, who didn't stop talking long enough to take a breath.

"The dining hall's that way. Breakfast is served from five-thirty to seven, lunch from eleven-thirty to one and dinner from six to seven-thirty. Social hour starts at five. 'Course, if you're hungry, Cook's always got a pot of stew or chili on the stove."

"I'll remember that."

Ty didn't anticipate doing much socializing during his four-week stay. He was here to rope. Though competent in other rodeo events, steer wrestling and team roping mostly, tie-down roping was what he excelled at.

Make that *had* excelled at. Everything had changed last December.

Stick escorted him to a long counter resembling a hotel registration desk, only on a much simpler scale. "You in there, Adele?" he called.

Ty caught a glimpse of a desk with a phone and computer through the open door behind the counter.

When no one answered, Stick tapped the

bell on the counter. It promptly dinged. "Huh." He pushed his cowboy hat back, revealing a shock of red hair, and scratched his forehead. "Guess she's not here."

"We can come back," Ty offered, in no hurry to meet the owner and manager of Cowboy College.

In the next instant, he mentally kicked himself. He hadn't come all this way to chicken out at the last minute.

"But we have to get the key to your guest cabin. How else you gonna unpack your stuff?"

"It'll wait," Ty assured him. The poor kid was trying so hard and deserved a break. "How 'bout we head to the barn and unload my horse. Maybe Adele will show up by the time we're done."

Stick immediately brightened. "Sure thing," he said, only it sounded more like "shore" thing.

Back outside, they hopped in Ty's truck, and Stick directed him down the dirt road to a row of three barns. Across the open area in front of them was a large arena complete with holding pens, boxes, chutes, bleachers and an announcer's stand. A handful of riders were honing their roping skills with the help of some wranglers. Situated behind the barns were two smaller arenas, a pair of round pens, and endless acres of fenced pastures in which dozens of horses grazed on fresh spring grass. About a half mile beyond that, at the base of a valley, afternoon sunlight glinted off a large pond. .

"How's the fishing?" Ty asked.

"Plenty of bass and bluegills. But if you're hankering for some serious fly-fishing, Little Twister Creek's the place to go. It's not far, about a mile or two from here. My cousin and I go every chance we get."

"You up for some company sometime?"

Stick's face exploded into a huge grin. "Just name the day." As they approached the row of barns, he indicated the largest one. "Here we are."

Ty pulled up in front of an old-fashioned hitching post and parked. His horse, Hamm, greeted him with a shrill whinny and a bang on the trailer sidewall when he went around the back and unlatched the gate. Eager to be free after the long drive, the large gelding piled out of the trailer. Once on solid ground, he raised his head high, took in his new surroundings and whinnied again. Mares with young foals in the far pasture ran to the fence for a closer look at the newcomer.

"He's a beaut!" Stick gazed at Hamm admiringly.

"That he is." Holding on to the lead rope with one hand, Ty patted the horse's neck. Plain old sorrel didn't begin to describe Hamm. With four perfectly matched white stockings and a three-inch-wide blaze running down the entire length of his face, he was striking.

"Bet he can chase calves down like lightning streakin' across a meadow."

"He's fast all right." Ty didn't elaborate. His problem, the reason he'd come to Cowboy College, had nothing to do with Hamm and everything to do with him.

"This way." Stick started toward the barn opening. After several steps, he turned, gave Ty's horse another adoring once-over and whistled low. "That big boy can sure walk out."

The barn housed at least forty horses. Every one of them charged to the door of their stall and hung their head out to observe the visitors. A few of the braver ones stretched their neck out to either sniff Hamm or give his rump a quick nip. Ty assumed some of the horses belonged to Cowboy College and the rest to guests like himself.

Midway down the aisle, Stick stopped and opened the door of an empty stall. "Here you go."

Being accustomed to traveling, Hamm entered his new quarters without balking. He quickly inspected the stall's perimeter, then buried his head in the feed trough. It was empty, and a second later his head shot up in obvious displeasure.

Given it was late afternoon, Ty supposed the stable hands would be feeding soon. Still, he asked, "You got a little grain or pellets we can give him until I go over his diet with the barn manager?" Hamm liked to eat, and a snack would help him adjust to his new surroundings.

"Be right back." Stick took off and promptly returned with a small bucket of oats.

Fifteen minutes later Ty and Stick were parking his trailer behind the barn. When they were done, Ty pulled his truck around front.

Stick sat forward in the passenger seat. "There's Adele." He hitched his chin toward the arena. "Come on, you can meet her."

Horses and their riders had gathered at the south end of the arena. Ty picked out a trim young woman astride a stout paint mare, a blond braid snaking down her back from beneath her battered cowboy hat. Despite the distance, he recognized her immediately. No surprise; he'd been staring at pictures of her on Cowboy College's website for weeks while deciding to come or not.

"She looks busy."

"Naw." Stick dismissed his concern with a wave. "She won't mind."

They selected a spot along the fence and settled in to watch, their forearms resting on the top rail.

"Hey, folks."

Stick's friendly greeting was returned by all except Adele. She was preoccupied with lining her horse up in the box. The mare, obviously new at tie-down roping, didn't like being enclosed in such a cramped space. She danced nervously, snorting and pulling on the bit. With firm hands and a honeyed voice, Adele brought the animal under control.

"Good girl." She placed the pigging string in her mouth, checked her rope and shifted in the saddle. Ty knew she would cue the wrangler manning the chute only when she and the horse were completely ready. That moment came a second later.

"Go!"

The wrangler slid open the gate, and the

calf bolted for freedom, running in a straight line away from the chute. Adele's horse might not have much experience, but its instincts were right on the money. The mare exploded from the box at a full gallop, following the calf with the persistence of a heat-seeking missile. Adele's arm came up. In the next instant, she threw her rope. The noose landed right where it should, squarely on the calf's horns, and she leaped from the saddle even before the mare had come to a complete stop.

Ty watched, completely captivated as she raced to the calf and dropped it effortlessly to the ground, securing its legs with the pigging string. She worked efficiently, not a single motion wasted. And yet there was a natural, fluid gracefulness about her.

It was then Ty noticed the mare. Rather than backing up and stretching the rope taut, as was her job, she moved aimlessly, allowing the rope to hang loosely. The lack of assistance, however, didn't appear to hamper Adele's performance. She threw her hands in the air, signaling she was done—in less than eight seconds, according to Ty's internal stopwatch. The students watching at the end of the arena broke into applause. He and Stick joined them.

Stick beamed. "Isn't she something?"

"Pretty good." Ty rocked back on his heels, absorbing what he'd just seen and thinking how much he hated admitting his sister might be right about Cowboy College.

Adele stood, exhibiting that same dancer's grace from earlier. The calf, now free, trotted off, only to be rounded up by one of the wranglers. Suddenly, Adele turned and glanced in Ty's direction. Their gazes connected, and the same recognition he'd experienced when he first saw her was reflected in her dark green eyes.

"Glad to see you made it, Mr. Boudeau. I'm Adele Donnelly."

"Glad to be here."

"Did you get your horse situated?"

"Stick's taken fine care of us."

At the compliment, Stick puffed up his skinny excuse for a chest. "Ty still needs to get checked in."

"I'll be up to the main lodge in a bit."

She walked over to her horse, calmly collecting her rope and winding it into a coil. With the ease and confidence of a practiced athlete, she swung up into the saddle and rode out of the arena.

Ty stared after her. Despite hearing of her

skill, he'd half expected—make that half hoped—the stories about her to be hype.

They weren't.

Adele Donnelly could not only show him a thing or two about a sport in which he'd been a top World contender mere months ago, she could quite possibly beat the pants off him.

"Hey, Dellie." Adele's grandfather joined her behind the registration counter. "What are you doing?"

"Hi, Pop." She straightened from her hunched position and rolled her cramped shoulders. "I'm just going over these schedules."

"I heard Tyler Boudeau arrived."

"About an hour ago."

"You meet him yet?"

"Briefly, at the arena."

"Which cabin did you assign him?"

"Number twenty-two."

Pop grunted. "The honeymoon cabin is bigger."

"It's booked. Number twenty-two is our next largest cabin, and the view from the back balcony's the best on the ranch."

"It's kind of far from the barn."

She studied him curiously, wondering what was up.

He rarely concerned himself with a guest's accommodations, preferring to leave the administrative functions of the ranch and roping school to Adele. On most days, when his acute arthritis didn't confine him to bed or the couch, he could be found at the barns and arena, teaching classes, overseeing the livestock and supervising the ranch hands. He still put in a full day's work when he could, but the last few years he'd come to depend more and more on their barn manager to pick up the slack.

"So, what do you think of him?"

Adele paused before answering the question, unsure of her response. Having a professional roper stay at the ranch, particularly one of Ty Boudeau's caliber, was certainly a boon for business. But the explanation he'd given for his month-long stay, that of training his new horse, hadn't rung true.

"We exchanged only a few words, and those were pleasant enough."

"Humph." Pop seemed disappointed.

"He should be here any minute."

His eyebrows shot up, momentarily erasing the deep wrinkles creasing his brow. "You don't say?"

Adele almost laughed, with surprise, not humor. Her grandfather was starstruck and couldn't wait to meet their semifamous guest.

"In that case, guess I'll get me a cup of coffee in the kitchen and wait for him."

"Decaffeinated," Adele called after his retreating back, and resisted adding, "You know what your doctor said."

A few minutes later, she looked up from her work to see Ty stride through the lobby door. She had to admit he wasn't hard to look at. And taller than she'd expected. Picking up the house phone, she paged the kitchen and said, "Tell Pop he's here," when Cook answered.

Reaching the counter, Ty removed his cowboy hat, and an unruly lock of sandy-blond hair promptly fell across his tanned forehead. His attempts to push it off his face were wasted…and also charming.

"Welcome again, Mr. Boudeau." She gave him her best professional yet friendly smile.

"Please, call me Ty."

"And I'm Adele."

The registration process didn't take long. When she finished, she put together a stack of papers, including a brochure, maps of the ranch and the nearby town of Markton, the current week's schedule of classes and events and a list of rules and regulations.

"Please read through this the first chance you have." She pointed to the papers stapled together on top. "You can't begin using the facilities until we have a signed copy on file."

"Tell me, am I signing away all my rights?"

Adele thought she detected a twinkle of amusement in his dark brown eyes. Perhaps he wasn't all-business, as she'd first suspected.

"No. You're just agreeing to abide by the rules and regulations. Very standard stuff. We already have the liability waiver and insurance certificate you faxed last week."

Ty signed the form without reading it and slid the papers across the counter.

"Let me make you a copy." She went into the office, where she kept a desktop copier, and returned shortly. "Here you go."

"Thanks." Ty folded the sheets in thirds and slipped them in his shirt pocket, again without reading them.

Oh, well, she'd done all she could.

Her grandfather appeared from the entryway leading to the kitchen, his chronic limp barely noticeable for once.

"Hey there, young fellow." He extended his right hand. "I'm mighty glad to make your acquaintance."

"Mr. Donnelly." Ty's glance fell for the briefest of seconds on Pop's hand before clasping it in a firm shake. "It's a real honor to meet you, sir."

Adele liked that Ty didn't appear put off by her grandfather's missing right thumb, a casualty of a roping accident that had happened long before she was born.

"The honor's mine," Pop said. "I've been watching your career since you were competing in junior rodeo."

"And I've studied yours."

"You have to go back a lot of years for that." Pop laughed, but it was filled with warmth.

"I'm counting on you teaching me a thing or two while I'm here. It's one of the reasons I came."

Pop stood a little taller. Most of their guests were recreationists and wannabe cowboys. Some were high-school students hoping to eventually compete on the professional rodeo circuit. Almost none of them knew about her grandfather's once impressive and long-ago rodeo career. Not until they got here and saw the photos and framed buckles on the lobby wall.

"I doubt there's anything I can teach you." Pop chortled. "Now Adele here, she's likely to have a trick or two up her sleeve you can use."

"I saw her earlier at the arena," Ty said. "She's good."

"She's the best in the state, man or woman." Pop's voice rang with pride.

Adele loved her grandfather, but at the moment she wanted to cringe. "Mr. Boudeau is one of the best in the world, Pop."

"Doesn't mean he can't learn a thing or two from you."

"I agree," Ty answered good-naturedly. "Getting help, from both of you, is the reason I'm here."

Adele wondered if he'd added the "from both of you" for her grandfather's sake, considering how hesitantly the words had rolled off his tongue.

"Pop, why don't you show Mr. Boudeau to his cabin? You two can swap stories on the ride."

"Nothing I'd like better. Except I'm due to meet the boys in thirty minutes."

His regular Thursday-night poker game. She'd forgotten about that. "I'll call Stick."

"Adele, maybe you can take me?" One corner of Ty's mouth lifted in a grin. A very potent grin. "I'd be much obliged."

"Certainly."

"Good," Pop said, with more satisfaction than the situation called for. "That's settled, then."

As Adele left the lodge with Ty, she couldn't shake the feeling that her grandfather had set her up. She should be mad at him, but when she hopped onto the truck seat next to Ty, being mad was the furthest thing from her mind.

Ty slanted a glance at Adele, wondering what she was thinking. They'd both been relatively quiet during the five-minute drive through the main part of the ranch, except for the occasional item of interest she pointed out.

"Is this my home away from home?" he asked when she directed him to an attractive cabin atop a rise.

"Yes." She removed an old-fashioned hotel key from her pocket. No key cards for Cowboy College. "You'll love the view from the back patio."

They climbed out of the truck, and Adele led him along a split-fence-lined walkway to the front porch. Unlocking the cabin door, she swung it wide, and went ahead only when he indicated for her to precede him inside.

Ty took in the cabin's spacious and charmingly appointed interior, which appeared to have every amenity he could possibly want. "Very nice."

"If you aren't happy here, we can always move you to a different cabin."

"Are you kidding? This is great."

"It's a little far from the barn and arena." Adele walked over to the drapes on the other side of the living room and opened them, revealing a sliding glass door that looked out onto a calendar-perfect view of the nearby pond and distant mountains.

He joined her at the door and scanned the horizon. A glorious red sun was starting to dip behind one of the mountain peaks.

"It's worth the extra distance just for this."

Adele eased away from him, piquing his interest. Women generally acted the opposite, hanging all over him if possible. It was either a hazard or a perk of his profession, depending on a guy's perspective. Ty mostly found it wearisome. Except in Adele's case. Sharing the same air space with her had definitely been enjoyable.

Apparently not so much for her.

"There are two bedrooms," she said, walking past the fully equipped kitchenette. "The master and a small guest room. The couch also folds out into a bed. Your rental agreement allows for overnight guests up to three consecutive nights, but you have to report them."

"Dana will be glad to hear that." Was it his imagination or did a glint of curiosity flash in Adele's eyes? "My little sister's been bugging me to come here and take lessons from you."

"Oh, really? We'd love to have her," Adele said, so smoothly that Ty figured he'd been mistaken.

Perhaps because she was so different from the women he usually met, or that she was a roper like himself, he found himself trusting her. Enough to reveal the real reason he'd come to Cowboy College.

He hadn't expected he would, the idea of enrolling in a roping school for amateurs being hard to swallow. Taking instructions from a woman made it worse. But she'd impressed him in the arena, demonstrating a core of steel.

Like the one he had lost.

"It's not just my horse," he said abruptly. "It's me."

"What?" She turned to face him, her expression puzzled.

He cleared his throat, freeing the words stuck in it. "The horse I'd been riding the past four years suffered a fractured metacarpal last December in a fall. Right before the National Finals Rodeo. I was ranked second at the time."

"I know, I read about it in *Roper Sports News*."

"I lost more than a gold buckle and a title that day. Iron Grip Ropes had signed me for a sponsorship deal. A very lucrative sponsorship deal."

"Which was contingent on you winning," she correctly guessed.

"I competed on a friend's horse, but lost the championship by one-point-eight seconds." Ty swallowed. Six months later, the bitter defeat still stung. "I bought Hamm in February after an extensive search. He's an incredible horse. Big, athletic, strong, fast and smart as a whip. Everything I could want." Ty paused.

"What's wrong, then?"

"That one-point-eight seconds. No matter what I do, no matter how hard I train, whatever trick I try, I can't seem to perform any better on Hamm than I did on my friend's horse. And I don't know why."

"Sometimes the partnership between a rider and horse is off."

"I'm hoping that's all it is. Because the alternative, that I've somehow lost my competitive edge...well, let's just say it's not acceptable."

He went to Adele and took her hand in his. The calluses on her palm from years of roping were in stark contrast to the silky smooth skin on the back of her hand. *Like her*, he thought—tough on one side, soft on the other.

"This isn't easy for me to ask, Adele. But I need your help."

She gazed at their joined hands for several seconds, then lifted her eyes to his. "I'll do my best."

"Good. Because the Buffalo Bill Cody Stampede Rodeo is less than four weeks away, and I *have* to win."

Chapter 2

Adele stood with Pop on the fence beside the chute and watched Ty position his horse in the roping box. People who weren't involved in rodeoing had no idea how many hours were spent training for the sport by studying others from the sidelines.

"What do you think?" Pop asked.

"Good-looking horse."

"Real nice looking."

So was the rider, but Adele kept that opinion to herself. Ty sat tall in the saddle, his Stetson angled low over his eyes, his Western cut shirt stretched taut across his broad shoulders. She wondered if he'd object to having his picture taken for their next website updates.

Almost immediately, she changed her mind. Ty had come to Cowboy College because of a problem, one he hoped to correct. It would be thoughtless and insensitive of her to take advantage of his misfortune in order to advance the ranch.

Ready at last, Ty signaled the wrangler, who pulled back the gate on the chute and released the calf. Ty's run, over in the span of a few heartbeats, was a good one. Not, however, spectacular. And spectacular runs were needed to win World championships.

"What do you think his problem is?" Adele asked her grandfather as Ty exited the arena.

"Not saying yet." Pop waved to Ty and pointed at the box, indicating for him to take another run.

Ty's admiration of her grandfather yesterday afternoon wasn't unfounded. Pop had been National tie-down roping champion for three years straight in the late 1950s, and again in 1963, before permanently retiring. Granted, things were done a little differently in those days, but the basic sport had remained the same.

One aspect not the same was the popularity of tie-down roping. That had grown tremendously in recent years, especially among amateurs. Not only did horse people with an interest in roping participate, so did thrill-seekers looking to try something new, urbanites wanting to experience the cowboy life, and even companies offering team-building retreats for their employees.

The increase in popularity was what had given Adele the idea to start Cowboy College. Her business savvy combined with her grandfather's experience made a winning combination. Together they'd turned a run-down ranch into a thriving enterprise.

Seven Cedars hadn't always been in trouble. For three decades after her grandparents bought the place, they'd run a modestly successful cattle business. Then, during Adele's junior year at university, her grandmother had died unexpectedly from an aneurysm. Pop sank into grief, letting the ranch go. Adele's father wasn't able to leave his job and move his second family from Texas to tend the ranch. Until Adele arrived after graduation, no one realized how bad the situation at Seven Cedars, and Pop's depression, had gotten.

Cowboy College not only breathed new life

into the ranch, it gave her grandfather a purpose again. Within a year, they'd opened their doors, and had grown steadily in the six years since. Guests came from all over the country now, spending anywhere from a long weekend to weeks on end.

Ty Boudeau, however, was their first ever professional roper.

His horse, Hamm, lined up in the box with only the smallest amount of urging. "Go!" he shouted. As on the first run, the wrangler released the calf and Ty successfully roped it in a respectable time.

"He could do this all day and it wouldn't be any different," Adele commented.

"I'm afraid you're right." Pop rolled the toothpick stuck in his mouth from one side to the other. He was rarely without one since giving up chewing tobacco years earlier. Another of his doctor's mandates.

"The horse isn't taking one wrong step," Adele commented, "and Ty's doing exactly what he should be doing."

"But the magic just isn't happening."

"Could his problem be lack of confidence?"

Pop shrugged. "Possibly. Losing a world championship when you're as close as he was could set anyone back."

"Except Ty doesn't strike me as lacking confidence." *In or out of the arena*, thought Adele.

But then, he'd lost much more than the championship. Sponsorship deals, good ones, didn't grow on trees, and had launched more than one athlete on a successful post-competing career.

"You never know," Pop mused out loud. "He could be putting on a good front. My guess is it's the horse."

Adele shot her grandfather a sideways look. "You just agreed Hamm's a nice horse."

"But he isn't Ty's other horse. Don't get me wrong. The boy was always a good roper, one to watch since he began competing in junior rodeo. He didn't come on strong until four years ago, when he got that horse. It was a perfect partnership. Now he's lost that partner."

"I think Hamm has the potential to be every bit as good as Ty's other horse."

"Maybe even better."

Adele nodded in agreement. "He just has to realize that."

"I'm thinking he already does." Pop's expression became pensive. "Recovering from a loss isn't easy, be it someone you've loved or a dream you've held. Something inside dies. There's no miracle cure and no set timetable for recovery. Ty will come back when he's ready." Pop turned a fond smile on Adele. "Or when someone shows him the way."

She patted his hand in return, recalling their early days of Cowboy College. "You could be right."

Stepping off the fence, she pushed a damp strand of hair off her face. The temperature might be only in the low seventies, but the bright morning sun beat down on them, warming her through and through. "If he were anyone else but Ty Boudeau, I'd recommend the beginners' class. The best way to get to know your horse is by starting with the basics."

Pop also stepped off the fence. "Why not Ty?"

"He's…one of the best ropers out there. He doesn't need a beginners' class."

"Are you sure? Could be just the ticket."

"He'll laugh in our faces, then pack his bags."

"He won't laugh if he's committed." Pop moved the toothpick to the other side of his mouth. "And Ty strikes me as a man with a mission."

"Excuse me for disagreeing."

"Relax, Dellie. You know it's a good idea. Ty Boudeau has everything it takes to be the next World Champion. And when he is, he's gonna be thanking you and me."

"Okay," she grumbled. "But I'm not going to be the one to tell him he has to take the beginners' class. *You* are."

"Isn't this place great? My husband and I arrived just a few days ago. We've never been here before. Have you?"

The woman astride the horse standing beside Ty had been rambling nonstop for five minutes solid, not caring if he answered her question or not before going on to the next one.

It was different being around people who didn't recognize him. Different and unsettling. When had he become so accustomed to the attention?

"How'd you get into roping? My husband rodeoed some when he was growing up. We saw a show on cable TV about couples roping, and decided to give it a try. And now we're hooked. Me, not so much."

The woman paused to take a breath. Ty used the lull to observe Adele.

She stood on the ground giving instructions to the group, which was comprised of about a dozen beginner ropers. Ty only half listened. He was quite familiar with the training technique she described—a fake calf head attached to a bale of hay and pulled by a wrangler driving an ATV. The group had assembled in one of the smaller arenas beside the barn, away from the ropers practicing in the main arena, in case the ATV spooked their horses.

"I can't believe I'm actually taking a roping class." The woman untangled her reins for the third time.

"Me, either."

When Pop had proposed the idea that Ty participate in the afternoon beginners' class, he'd balked. Then he learned Adele would be teaching it. That, and the arguments Pop had presented about getting back to basics, convinced Ty to give one—and *only* one—class a try. He told himself it wasn't because he found Adele attractive. Rather, he wanted to see if she could teach as well as she roped. His decision to remain at Cowboy College depended on the outcome.

She continued explaining how the wrangler would take off on the ATV, and that the riders should allow their horses to follow the calf head and bale of hay, rather than attempt to direct them.

Yeah, yeah. Ty suppressed a yawn.

His cell phone rang a minute later, coming just when he thought he'd reached his boredom threshold. Unclipping the phone from his belt, he checked the screen. A photo of his younger sister appeared with her name above it.

"Sorry, I need to take this call," he told the students nearest him, and nudged Hamm into a fast walk away from the group. Stopping about twenty feet away, he answered the call. "Hey, Dana."

From his chosen spot, he could see Adele frowning at him. Too late, Ty realized there was probably something in the rules and regulations he hadn't yet read about no cell-phone calls during class. Oh, well, he'd already screwed up.

"How's it going, bro?"

"Not so great."

"Why?"

"Because I'm sitting here in a beginners' class."

"Really! Doing what? Showing the students how it's done?"

"No, attending. Actually, attending as little as possible."

"I guess a refresher course never hurts."

He should have figured Dana would agree with Pop's suggestion, being it was her idea to come to Cowboy College.

"Right. I could be doing this in my sleep."

"So prove it."

"You're not serious." He laughed.

"I am, Ty. You need to figure out what's not working, and fix it. Taking a beginner class might seem ridiculous, but you need a new perspective, and I'm all for trying anything. You should be, too, if you want to win that championship."

Ty tamped down his rising annoyance. It had been a long time since anyone had lectured him. A long time since he'd felt he deserved a lecture.

A quick glance at Adele confirmed yet another talking-to might be in store for him. She looked about as happy with him as his sister sounded.

"This isn't easy for me, Dana." The admission came with an uncomfortable tightening in his gut.

"I know, honey. But I'm one of the people who has your back, remember?"

"And I appreciate it."

"You couldn't have two better experts there."

"I agree with you about Pop Donnelly. And I wouldn't mind half so much if he was teaching the class."

"What's wrong with Adele Donnelly?"

There was nothing wrong with her that Ty could see. It was his ego having the problem. Granted, he'd asked for her help yesterday, but that was in a weak moment. This morning, when he'd faced himself in the bathroom mirror, he wished he'd asked Pop for help instead.

It wasn't too late. He'd get through this one class and seek out the older man. Maybe then he wouldn't feel like so much of a loser. Or have an entire group of people witnessing his shame.

"You practice with a woman roper," Dana prompted.

"It's different with you."

"Because I'm not competing against you in the same sport?"

"Yikes." Ty grimaced. "That smarts."

"Give Adele a chance before you hightail it out of there."

How did his sister know he'd been contemplating leaving? "Fine. I promise to stay another couple days."

"You said a month." Her tone dared him to defy her.

"Okay, okay. You win."

"Call me if you need anything."

"I will." They disconnected after saying goodbye.

Ty silenced his cell phone and walked Hamm over to the group, smiling apologetically to his classmates and Adele, who blatantly ignored him. All right, he deserved that. Leaning forward and propping a forearm on the saddle horn, he made an effort to really listen to her. After several minutes passed, he had to agree she knew her stuff. She certainly had the attention of all the students.

"Are we ready to try? Who wants to go first?"

Hands shot into the air, none of them Ty's.

"All right, how about you, Mike?" She picked the husband of the woman Ty'd been talking to earlier.

He sat quietly on Hamm, watching Mike and the others take their turns one by one. He easily and quickly spotted the errors with each student. Adele did, too, and patiently explained it to them in laymen's terms the students could comprehend. When everyone had done it, Adele's gaze landed on him.

"You're up next, Ty."

He moved into position behind the bale of hay. Hamm pawed the ground, far more eager to get started than his owner.

"Wait. We're going to do this a little differently with you. Put up your rope."

"My rope?"

"Then drop your reins and kick your feet out of the stirrups."

"You're kidding."

"No hands, no legs."

"Why?" he asked.

"You don't think you can stay seated?" Her green eyes flashed up at him.

He attached his lasso to his saddle with the rope strap. "Ma'am, I can break a green horse riding bareback and with one hand tied behind my back."

"Then this should be a cakewalk for you." She stepped away from him.

With a shrug of his shoulders, his hands resting on his thighs and his legs dangling, he waited for the wrangler to take off on the ATV.

"One more thing," Adele said, the lowered brim of her cowboy hat partially hiding her face. "You have to do it with your eyes closed."

"Excuse me?"

"Eyes closed, Mr. Boudeau."

Was she smiling?

Ty decided to go along with her rather than put up a fight. He'd promised Dana, and besides, the students might learn something from watching him.

"Go!" he told the wrangler.

Hamm took off after the bale of hay as if it were the real thing. Because the wrangler didn't drive the ATV very fast, Hamm's gait was an easy lope rather than a full-out gallop, as it would be in the arena.

Ty set down deep in the saddle, adjusting himself to the horse's rhythm. Trying to, he amended. It wasn't as easy as he might have guessed. Not with his eyes closed and his legs dangling. As the driver zigzagged, mimicking the course a calf might take, Ty felt—*really* felt—the nuances of Hamm's muscles bunching and releasing when he changed directions. Ty shifted accordingly, to compensate for the horse's movements, thinking about it rather than doing it instinctively as he should.

After thirty feet, the wrangler slowed to a stop. Hamm also slowed. Opening his eyes, Ty used the pressure of his legs to guide his horse in a circle and back toward the group. Once there, he stopped and rubbed his neck, contemplating what had just happened.

"You look perplexed," Adele said, studying him.

"Not that so much," he answered.

She'd put him through a very basic exercise, one, he realized in hindsight, he should have tried himself. Perhaps if he had, the results wouldn't be quite so startling.

Ty trusted himself as a rider. What he'd learned today was that he didn't trust Hamm. Not entirely and not enough. His other horse's accident had robbed Ty of that vital component to a successful rider-horse partnership, and the tiny fear that it would happen again was causing him to hold back.

"Ty?" Adele asked.

He grinned suddenly and waved to the wrangler to come back around.

"I want to go again."

"Hey, Adele, hold on a minute."

Hearing her name, she stopped and turned to see Ty hurrying after her.

Uh-oh. He was probably annoyed at her for what she'd pulled on him during class earlier. Squaring her shoulders, she waited for him to catch up, committed to defending her actions.

"Can I help you with something?" She smiled, pretending she didn't notice the Ben Affleck–like perfection of Ty's strong, dimpled chin or the fluttering in her middle that ogling his chin caused. "Perhaps a copy of the rules and regulations you obviously lost."

"I guess I deserve that." He returned her smile with a healthy dose of chagrin. "No more phone calls. You have my word."

She was glad to see he didn't take offense at her more-serious-than-humorous jest. Rules were rules, in place for a reason, and Ty Boudeau didn't get to break them just because he was a professional roper.

"You're allowed one mistake before we start giving demerits. Ten demerits, however, and you're kicked off the ranch."

His startled expression was so comical, she almost laughed. "I'm joking."

The hint of a twinkle lit his eyes. "You're good, you know."

"I've had a lot of practice keeping unruly students in line."

"No denying I'm one of those unruly students in need of lining out, but that's not what I meant."

"Oh?"

"You're good at spotting what a person's doing wrong. Me included."

She knitted her brows in confusion. "I didn't notice you doing anything wrong."

"Maybe not exactly. But the exercise helped me understand some things about myself. Things that need fixing."

"Not many competitors at your level would admit to that. I'm impressed."

"Don't be. I'm usually thickheaded. A good suggestion could be driving a Mack truck straight at me, and I'd ignore it."

"I'll remember that next time."

He moved closer. "I just wanted to thank you for the help."

"You're welcome." She worried that he was going to take her hand again. Relief flooded her when he didn't. One intimate encounter was more than she could handle. "Have a productive remainder of your day, Mr. Boudeau."

"If you don't mind, I'd like to pick your brain sometime when you have a minute."

She debated refusing his request. In the end, she decided to grant it. He was a paying guest, after all, and part of the fees they charged entitled students to "pick her brain," as he said.

"I'm heading over to check on one of our expectant mares. You can come with me if you like."

His dark eyes, arresting to begin with, lit up. "I would."

"I'm not keeping you from anything important, am I?"

He fell step in beside her. "Only the horde of adoring female fans waiting for me in the lobby."

She momentarily faltered. "If you have to go…"

"I'm kidding." He flashed her his heart-stopping grin.

It appeared she was just as gullible as him.

He surprised her during their walk with the questions he asked, which were detailed and thought provoking. Did tie-down straps really help horses stop faster, or hinder them? How did she feel about the new Professional Cowboy Association regulations, and did they affect her teaching methods? What kind of personal fitness regime, if any, did she recommend for her students?

More than once, Adele found herself examining the techniques of roping from a different and enlightening perspective.

"Here's where Pop and I keep our private stock," she told Ty when they entered the smallest of the ranch's three barns. At the end of the aisle, they came to a double-wide stall separated from the other horses by twenty feet and a six-foot wall.

"And this is Crackers," Adele said by way of introduction.

Upon seeing her, the heavily pregnant mare nickered softly and lumbered over from the corner where she'd been standing, to hang her shaggy head over the stall door.

Adele stroked the animal's neck. "She was my first barrel-racing horse. Gosh, was that really fourteen years ago?"

"Did you compete professionally?" Ty asked. He stood beside her, his elbow propped on the stall door.

"A little in college."

"Any good?"

"All right."

"Why'd you quit?"

She absently combed her fingers through Crackers's mane. "I came here after graduation to help Pop with the ranch. He'd turned seventy, and his arthritis was getting bad. He needed help, and I needed a job." She didn't mention her grandmother's death. "I've always loved Seven Cedars, and spent a lot of time here when I was growing up."

"Did your parents rodeo?"

"My dad. Though he never did all that well, and moved to Texas years ago. My mom traveled the rodeo circuit considerably longer than Dad, but not to compete."

Adele didn't elaborate. Despite Ty's friendliness, she wasn't ready to confess that her mother had taken up with whatever cowboy would have her, dropping Adele off with her grandparents if her father wouldn't have her. As her mother aged and her looks faded, those cowboys went from being competitors to bullfighters to stock handlers. In between men, she'd find a small place to rent for herself and Adele, but only until another man came along. For a young girl feeling unloved and unwanted, Seven Cedars became a haven in an otherwise turbulent childhood.

"So, Pop taught you to rope."

"He was a man ahead of his time. In those days, women didn't rope. Period." She opened the stall door and went in to give Crackers a closer inspection.

"She looks close," Ty observed.

"Soon." The foal had dropped considerably in the last week, but otherwise, Crackers showed no signs of delivering. "She's due this week."

"Her first?"

"Second. Up until a few years ago, we used her steadily for beginner students. When her stamina began to fade, we decided to breed her." Adele patted Crackers's rump, then left the stall and shut the door behind her. "She's got good lines, and she's a good mama."

"And she's your first horse."

"Pop bought her for me when I was a freshman in high school. There were always plenty of horses to ride wherever I lived, but she was the first one that was truly mine." Latching the stall door, she met Ty's gaze. "Cook will be serving dinner soon, and I need to get back to my office first."

"Will I see you in the dining hall?"

"Absolutely."

Adele made a point of sharing dinner each evening with the students, often moving from one table to another. That way, she got to know them on a more personal level. Breakfast and lunch, however, were hit-or-miss and often consumed on the run.

At the entrance to the barn, she and Ty

separated, each heading to their own vehicle. Hers was parked closer, and she hesitated before climbing in, stilled by the sight of Ty striding to his truck.

It had been a very long time since Adele had met a man who gave her that uncomfortable yet deliciously thrilling feeling every time she got within ten feet of him.

She silently warned herself to proceed with caution. Ty Boudeau had all the makings of a heartbreaker, and as much as she might want to get to know him on a more "personal level," she was far better off keeping her distance.

Men who spent inordinate amounts of time on the road didn't make good husbands. It was one of the many lessons her parents' failed marriage and her mother's endless stream of lovers had taught Adele.

Chapter 3

Ty drove through the small town of Markton, the closest community to Cowboy College. It could hardly be described as a metropolis, but he liked its grassroots country charm, its one stoplight at the intersection of Main Street and Brown, and the way everybody waved at everybody else.

Markton was a far cry from Santa Fe, where he'd grown up. He couldn't say *lived* because once he'd left home to rodeo full-time, he traveled six to nine months a year. When he needed to crash for a while, he stayed at his older sister's place. His fifth-wheel trailer parked behind the barn was, sad to say, the closest thing he had to a permanent residence.

He drove along Main Street at the posted speed of thirty-five, enjoying his free afternoon and taking in the various sights. The Spotted Horse Saloon. The feed store. Bush's General Store. The elementary school. The barbershop and its counterpart, Goldie's Locks and Nail Salon.

He'd often thought he might like to settle down in a town like Markton, and as he drove through it—end to end in less than five minutes—he contemplated where to stop first.

The feed store, an always familiar stomping ground, looked to have possibilities. Ty pulled into an empty space across from a sign advertising a popular brand of dog food. Inside the store, he was greeted by the middle-aged man behind the counter, whose double take was almost comical.

"Ty Boudeau?" he asked with raised brows.

"On a good day," Ty joked.

"We heard you were in town." The man came around from behind the counter carrying a pen and piece of paper. "Name's Henry Parkman."

"Pleased to meet you."

"If it's not too much trouble, the wife would sure love to have your autograph."

"No trouble."

It felt good being asked. The requests for autographs had tapered off since he'd lost at Nationals. Ty preferred to think it was because he hadn't been competing of late, not that he'd fallen from grace.

As he scribbled his name on the notepad, Henry Parkman produced his cell phone, held it at arm's reach, leaned in close and snapped a picture of him and Ty.

"For the wife." He grinned sheepishly. "Anything special I can help you with today?"

"Just browsing."

"Holler if you need me," he said to Ty, returning to his place behind the cash register.

Ty gravitated to the back of the store where the saddles and a rather impressive assortment of lariats hung on the wall. Though he wasn't in the market for another one, he removed several from the wall display and tested them for weight and flexibility.

For reasons he chose not to address, he avoided the Iron Grip Ropes—though it probably had something to do with the face smiling at him from the rope's cardboard wrapper.

Garth Maitland. The man who'd beat out Ty for the championship last December.

"Mr. Boudeau?" The cracking voice belonged to a teenager who bore a striking resemblance to Stick.

"Hi."

"Hate to bother you, sir," he said, his exceptionally large Adam's apple bobbing as he talked, "but could I trouble you for an autograph?"

"Are you by chance related to Stick over at Cowboy College?" Ty asked as he signed the kid's ball cap with a black marker.

The teen's eyes went wide. "He's my cousin."

"Well, he's a pretty good worker. But don't tell him I said so."

"I—I won't," the kid stammered, and made a beeline for the door.

Ty wasn't in the market for a new pair of boots, either, but he checked out the selection just for something to do. The front-door buzzer went off every few minutes as customers came and left. Deciding he could possibly use a new leather belt, he picked one out and headed to the counter.

While he completed his purchase, the door buzzer went off again. Bidding the store owner goodbye, he turned…and came face-to-face with Adèle.

"Oh!" She drew back. "Hello. I didn't know you were here."

"Just seeing what the town has to offer." He glanced at the attractive young woman beside Adèle, whose stylish clothes and painful looking four-inch heels were more suited to a stroll down Hollywood Boulevard than Main Street in Markton. "I'm Ty Boudeau."

"This is my friend Reese Carter. She's engaged t-to…" Adèle stammered, then recovered. "She lives on the ranch next door."

Ty's chest suddenly constricted, and he cautioned himself not to jump to conclusions. Markton boasted more than one rodeo family; Seven Cedars had more than one neighbor.

"Nice to meet you," he said, and shook the hand Reese offered. "Are you ladies in the market for horse pellets?"

"We were just killing a little time before going for lunch at the Spotted Horse."

"They serve food?"

"Surprisingly good food." Reese smiled brightly.

She sure didn't look as if she'd grown up on a ranch, not with her high heels and the designer sunglasses propped on her head.

"Well, it was nice running into you." Adele looked ready to bolt, and clamped on to her friend's arm. "See you later at the ranch."

"Would you like to join us for lunch?" Reese asked.

"I'm sure he's busy," Adele cut in before Ty could answer.

Because she seemed in such an all-fired hurry to get away from him, he answered, "I'd like that very much. Appreciate the invitation."

Adele's mouth, usually lush and pretty, tightened.

Finding her discomfort amusing, Ty followed the ladies to the door and held it open for them. They crossed the street at the corner and went up half a block to the saloon entrance.

Inside, Reese informed the hostess her fiancé would be joining them.

"I'll show him to your table."

"That won't be necessary." Reese peered past the hostess, her face alight. "Here he comes now."

Everyone looked over to see a handsome cowboy making his way toward them, his swagger confident.

The same anxiety that had gripped Ty

that first day at Cowboy College, the one he thought he'd successfully conquered, returned with a vengeance. Too late, he realized his mistake—he'd misread Adele completely. At the least, he should have asked Reese her fiancé's name before barging in on her and Adele's lunch date.

Then he wouldn't be stuck sitting across the table from the man who had beat him in team and tie-down roping last December, stealing the title of World Champion and the Iron Grip sponsorship deal from him.

Each bite of Ty's Swiss-cheese-and-mush-room burger tasted like paste and sat in his stomach like a lead ball. He couldn't fault Garth Maitland for his unappetizing meal. The guy had been nothing but decent all during lunch. He always was, even when Ty lost to him at Nationals.

Until then, Ty and Garth had been friendly rivals, getting along well, real well even, when they weren't competing. Not the same could be said when they were in the arena. Both of them were out to win, and a mutual liking and respect of each other's abilities went only so far. After losing the title, Ty had kept his distance from Garth. Not because he resented the man; Garth had won fair and square. The problem was Ty's, who felt he was staring his personal failings square in the face each time he looked at Garth.

The lunch conversation, stilted at first, soon settled into a congenial rhythm, carried mostly by his companions. Ty injected a comment every now and then just to keep anyone from noticing his discomfort.

Except one person did.

"I'm sorry," Adele whispered under her breath, when Garth and Reese were busy speaking to each other and momentarily ignoring them. "I tried to—"

"Not your fault," Ty whispered back. They were seated together in the booth, the only positive thing about lunch as far as he was concerned. "It's okay."

"Really?" She appeared genuinely distraught.

He flashed his best interview smile, hoping to reassure her. "Really."

She'd tried to avoid this disaster earlier at the feed store. He had no one to blame but himself.

"What brings you to Cowboy College, Ty?" Reese asked, her demeanor curious but friendly.

Instantly, silence descended on the table. Adele gnawed her lower lip. Garth's eyebrows raised in curiosity.

Ty got annoyed—with himself and the situation. Okay, he'd lost the world championship title and a profitable sponsorship deal. To the man with whom he'd just eaten lunch. No reason for everyone to act as if he had an incurable disease.

"I apologize if I said something wrong." Reese looked contrite.

"You didn't." Ty gave her credit for not ignoring the sudden tension. "I came to Cowboy College for Adele's help with my new horse." The glossed-over explanation sounded better than the truth.

"It was a shame about your other horse," Garth said sympathetically. "And bad timing."

"It was. But these things happen."

"They do. My old partner fell and busted his kneecap last September. He won't be competing again until this fall, and even that's iffy."

"Here's to this season." Ty lifted his mug of beer in a toast.

"To this season," Garth repeated, and lifted his own, a glint in his eyes. He was obviously looking forward to the next time they went up against each other.

Determination surged inside Ty. Residing next door to his rival might have some advantages. At the very least, the constant reminder would help motivate him and keep him focused on his goal.

Reese's glance traveled from one man to the other. "Is something going on here I don't get?"

Garth chuckled.

Ty wanted to but wasn't able to let his guard down enough to explain.

The remainder of their meal went well, until it came time to pay the server.

"I've got it." Ty reached for the bill.

"No problem." Garth beat him to the punch by a scant second. "I already told the waitress lunch was on me." He signed the slip with a flourish.

"All right. I'll buy next time."

"Deal." Garth grinned, and for a moment they were friends again.

Outside the saloon, they made plans to go their separate ways.

"You need to head back to the ranch right away?" Reese asked Adele.

"If you don't mind. I've got a bunch of work at the office stacked up."

"It's Sunday. Don't you ever take any time off?"

"I just did."

"You work way too hard," Reese scolded, and slung an arm around Adele's shoulders. "Come on, we'll drive you home."

"She can ride with me," Ty offered. He'd assumed Adele had driven herself, or he would have offered earlier.

"You don't have to," she answered a little too quickly.

"No problem. I'm going that way."

"I hate cutting your trip to town short."

"You're not. I was just thinking of heading back to the ranch." In truth, he'd been planning on driving down the road to Little Twister Creek and the fishing spot Stick had mentioned earlier. Noting Adele's hesitancy, Ty couldn't help himself and pressed the point, if only to see if she'd rather inconvenience her friends than ride with him.

"Why don't you come by one day for a visit?" Garth suggested. "Have a look around."

Ty had seen pictures of Garth's place in various rodeo publications. It was a roper's dream. Part of him wanted to go, just to check out the setup and salivate. The other part of him resisted. He would, after all, be walking into the enemy's camp.

"Thanks. I may take you up on that one day."

"Bring your horse. When you and Adele have worked out the kinks," he added.

Ty bristled. With competitiveness, not anger. He recognized a challenge when it was issued, and would like nothing better than to take Hamm over to Garth's and show him what he could expect to see on the circuit next month.

"I'll do that. Soon."

"I'm looking forward to it."

"I don't know about you," Reese said to Adele with exaggerated weariness, "but I've had just about as much testosterone as I can handle in one day." She looped her arm through Garth's. "It was really nice meeting you, Ty. And I do hope you'll come for a visit. With or without your horse. Bye, sweetie." She blew Adele a kiss. "Call me tomorrow."

"You okay?" Ty asked Adele as they were heading to his truck. "You've been awfully quiet."

"A little tired. I ate too much at lunch."

"We can walk a bit if you want."

"I really should get back to work."

He was pretty certain there was more to her subdued mood, but didn't ask, opening the passenger side door instead.

"Sorry about me and Garth back there," he said as he drove. The ranch was only about a fifteen-minute ride from town. Ty didn't intend to spend it all in silence. "We probably got a little carried away."

"It's understandable. All things considered, I think you two behaved quite well."

"Meaning he could have rubbed his championship belt buckle in my face?"

"That, and you could have retaliated with something equally petty. It had to be hard for you, sitting there, pretending you weren't bothered."

"Not as hard as watching him win last December. You have no idea how much I wanted his rope to land short that day."

"I do," she said absently, staring out the window. "I've watched men compete in roping for years, and known that no matter how good I was, no matter how hard I trained, I'd never be allowed to compete against them."

"Do you want to?"

"I do and have. In local jackpots where

women are allowed to enter. But it's not the same as a professional rodeo."

"You're the exception. Not many women can go head-to-head with a man in this sport."

"Not yet."

Ty had to smile. He had no doubt if a member of the fairer sex could break into professional tie-down roping and pave the path for others, it would be Adele Donnelly.

Which was why he should probably give her every opportunity to help him with his problem.

"Selfishly," he admitted, "I'm glad you're not competing professionally."

"Why's that?"

"Because after the last few days, I'm thinking you're the only person who can help me." Her expression softened. So did a place in Ty's heart. "Unless you think it's a conflict of interest. Garth's your neighbor and friend."

"No conflict. He understands business is business."

"Just out of curiosity, have you ever beaten him in a one-on-one match?"

Her green eyes sparkled. "Frequently."

Ty burst into the first true belly laugh he'd had in months.

Moments later, they pulled up in front of

the main lodge. He put the truck in Park but left the motor running.

"Thanks for the ride." Adele had her hand on the door handle but made no move to open it.

Was she also reluctant for their afternoon encounter to end?

"Thanks for letting me tag along during your lunch," Ty said.

"Are you serious? It couldn't have been that much fun for you."

"There were a few high spots." Like the seating arrangement.

"Next time I try to warn you—" she gave him a stern look "—pay attention."

"How 'bout next time we go to lunch just the two of us?"

The pause that followed lasted a little too long.

"I…uh…" She inhaled slowly and squared her shoulders. "Thank you for asking, but I don't date guests."

He hid his disappointment with a joke. "Is that one of those rules on the list I haven't read yet?"

"No, a personal one. Less messy that way when the guest leaves." Without another word, she pushed open the passenger door and hopped out, giving him the briefest of waves as she climbed the steps to the lodge entrance.

Her abrupt departure had Ty wondering if she'd been there and done that, and been left behind with a wounded heart.

And since he was leaving after the Buffalo Bill Cody Stampede, he certainly couldn't argue the logic behind her rule.

"What's wrong?"

"Nothing, Pop." Adele had practically steamrolled her grandfather in her haste to get inside.

"You sure?" He studied her with concern.

She suspected he'd been watching her and Ty from the lobby window. "Absolutely. Why would you think there was?" She made her way around the registration counter and into the sanctuary of her small office.

Pop followed her, shutting the door behind them except for a narrow crack—just in case someone rang the bell.

"You're upset, and Ty looked none too happy, either."

She was never any good at hiding her feelings. "Reese and I ran into him at the feed store. He wound up joining us for lunch. Garth was there, too."

Pop harrumphed. "Guess I can't blame the boy for being a touch prickly after that."

"Actually, he handled it pretty well." She gave her grandfather a brief account of the lunch.

"Then why are you acting like you two tangled? Is he mad about taking the beginner class?"

"Not at all."

Pop lowered himself carefully into the office's single visitor chair, wincing slightly. When he was settled, he let out a long groan. "Damn hip's giving me fits today. Must be the rain."

It hadn't rained in over two weeks and didn't remotely look like it was going to anytime soon. "You taking the new medicine your doctor prescribed?"

"Yes, and quit nagging me." They both knew he should have hip-replacement surgery, but Pop insisted he wasn't going under the knife unless it was a matter of life and death.

Adele thought his refusal had more to do with her than any fear of hospitals. He worried about leaving the entire responsibility of the ranch and Cowboy College to her.

"And quit changing the subject," he scolded.

"What?"

"From you and Ty." His wizened features softened. "You like him."

Hoping to distract her grandfather, she shook her mouse and roused her computer from its hibernation. "He's just another guest."

"You don't date enough. You need to get out and have a little fun now and then."

"I went to lunch today."

"With friends. That's not the same."

No? It had felt a little like a date. Part of the time, anyway.

"You've haven't gone out with anyone since that Joe kid from Phoenix."

"Yes, I have."

"When? Who?"

Adele searched her brain and came up blank. "I'm sure I have."

Pop just grunted. His way of saying he was right.

She skimmed the contents of her email inbox, hating to agree with her grandfather. Joe had been her last relationship, and it could hardly be called serious. In fact, none of her relationships since she'd graduated high school had been serious.

"Ty's a good man," Pop continued, oblivious to her diversion tactics. "And he's taken a shine to you. I can tell by how he looks at you."

"I'm not interested in him except as a guest of this ranch and a student in my class."

Pop chuckled. "I guess that's why you were walking away from him earlier like a bee flew up the back of your shirt."

"I was not!" Adele's heated denial was met with another grunt. She clicked on the unopened emails in earnest, ignoring her grandfather.

He abruptly sobered. "Is it because he's a professional roper?"

She didn't respond.

"They're not all bad," his said, his gravelly voice dropping in pitch.

"I know." She turned and gave him a soft smile. "But men like you are the exception, not the rule."

"It's been a lot of years, Dellie. Time you moved on. Put your parents and what they did behind you."

"I don't want to talk about them. Not now."

"Just because your mom and dad were

lousy parents is no reason to shut yourself off from love. I won't be around forever."

"Don't say that!"

"You need someone besides an old coot like me to dote on. A husband. Children."

"You're more than enough."

"Get to know Ty. Don't let him being a professional roper put you off."

Her grandfather had hit the nail on the head, and they both knew it. Work was simply an excuse. The main reason Adele didn't date much was because the vast majority of single men she met were unsuitable. Markton was a small town and the pickings slim to begin with. Making it worse, she didn't date employees or, as she'd told Ty, guests. Most others close to her age were either rodeo men or wannabe rodeo men.

After watching her parents destroy each other's lives *and* hers, she'd vowed not to become involved with anyone remotely connected with "the business."

"He's leaving in a few weeks, Pop. Even if I wanted to give him a shot, I wouldn't."

Before her grandfather could comment, the bell on the reception counter rang. Adele sprang to her feet and called, "Be right there."

As there were no new guests scheduled to

arrive today, she fully expected to see one of their current students standing at the counter, waiting to inform her of a need. At the sight of the lone, middle-aged woman wheeling one small suitcase, Adele came to a sudden stop, every thought flying instantly out of her head.

"Who is it?" Pop asked, hobbling out the office door. He, too, drew up short. But unlike Adele, he wasn't at a loss for words. "What the hell are you doing here?"

Adele wanted to know the same thing.

"Oh, Pop," Lani Donnelly chirped. "Is that anything to say to your daughter-in-law?" She turned to Adele, a too-sunny-to-be-real smile on her face. "Don't just stand there, baby girl, come give your mom a hug."

Chapter 4

Adele didn't move right away. She couldn't. Waves of hurt, anger and resentment hit her all at once and kept her rooted in place. She was vaguely aware of a guest coming out of the business center and leaving through the lobby entrance. She was *acutely* aware of her grandfather standing beside her. For a man with debilitating arthritis, his spine had snapped as straight and rigid as an iron bar.

"Please, baby girl." The pleading in her mother's voice penetrated the haze surrounding Adele.

She shored up her defenses, only to discover they weren't as impenetrable as she'd hoped. The sad and neglected little girl inside her still longed for the comfort of her mother's arms and the reassurance that she was loved.

"You okay, Dellie?"

At Pop's question, Adele glanced down, to see that her hands were shaking.

"I'm fine." And she was fine. Pulling herself together, she wrung the tremors from her fingers and raised her chin. No matter what, her mother wasn't going to hurt her again. Not after Adele had worked so hard to create a good life for herself.

"Hello, Mom."

They each took a step, then two, and met in the middle. The hug Adele offered was reserved. Not so for her mother, who clung to her, then burst into great racking sobs.

Adele wanted to remained unaffected, but couldn't. Years of mistrust and disappointment, however, enabled her to extract herself from her mom's desperate grasp.

"What's wrong?" she asked.

"Nothing." Lani dabbed at her eyes. "I'm just so happy to see you. It's been months."

Almost two years, but Adele didn't bother correcting her.

They were about the same height and had

once possessed similar figures. A weight loss during the last two years had left Lani painfully thin. Combined with her rough-around-the-edges appearance, she looked years older than her actual age. Her green eyes, highlighted with too much makeup, darted around the lobby with the desperation of a starving animal seeking its next meal.

"You should have called to let us know you were coming." Adele struggled to keep bitterness from creeping into her voice. Her mother may have hit rock bottom—the only reason Adele could think of to explain the unexpected visit—but that didn't erase all the bad memories.

"The battery died on my cell phone, and I haven't had a chance to replace it."

She was lying. Adele could feel it in her gut. Her mother had probably been unable to pay her bill without the help of a man.

Was else was she covering up?

"You look good, Pop." Lani smiled at Adele's grandfather, though her eyes were still filled with tears.

"You don't." Leave it to Pop to cut to the chase.

"This last year's been pretty hard on me." She swallowed.

He hobbled closer. "Is that why you just showed up out of the blue?"

"I, ah…"

One of the housekeeping staff entered the lobby pushing a cart laden with cleaning supplies, fresh linens and a vacuum. After a hesitant glance at them, she changed direction and went into the TV lounge to begin her work.

Lani rolled her suitcase from one side to the other. Uncertainty clouded her features, and she blurted, "I need a place to stay for a few days. Maybe a few weeks. I know it's a lot to ask, and Lord knows you have every reason turn me away, but I've got nowhere else to go. I'm willing to work off my room and board."

Adele took a step back, stunned by her mother's request. She didn't know what shocked her more—that her mother had the gall to show up unexpectedly and ask for a favor, a big one, or that she was actually willing to work. Lani hadn't voluntarily sought employment that Adele could recall.

"I don't know, Mom," she hedged. "We're kind of full right now."

"I can always sleep on your couch." The

offhand remark came across as desperate. "You'll hardly know I'm there. I swear."

Adele almost choked. Her mother sleeping on her couch? Not in this lifetime. "Mom—"

"She can stay in room nine." Pop stepped around Adele.

She started to protest, not wanting her mother anywhere near Seven Cedars, only to shut her mouth when Pop took hold of her mother's suitcase.

"Come on, we'll take you there now. Dellie, grab the key and bring the golf cart around."

Though they ran the ranch together, it technically belonged to Pop. Adele might disagree with his decision, and would tell him later when they were in private, but the choice to let Lani stay was his to make.

She promptly spun on her heels and fled to her office without glancing back.

In addition to eighteen fully equipped cabins, they had a building with nine hotel-like rooms behind the main lodge. Number nine was on the end, the smallest of the rooms, and contained only a twin bed. For that reason, it was usually vacant. The room had been reserved for the upcoming weekend, but the guest had canceled.

It looked to Adele as if they wouldn't be

renting number nine out even if they did get a last-minute request.

Removing the room and golf cart keys from a cabinet in her office, she exited the lodge through the kitchen's back door. The cart was parked under the large cedar tree where she'd last left it. She preferred driving ATVs, and used the golf cart mostly to transport guests and their luggage.

Not once had she imagined that her mother would ever be a guest.

The reason Lani had given for her unannounced visit didn't ring true. Though it was obvious she was in dire straits, Adele couldn't shake the sensation there was more going on than a run of bad luck. The question was what?

"Here we are," she announced when they pulled in front of room nine.

The three of them climbed out of the golf cart's one bench seat with noticeable relief. Pop insisted on removing Lani's bag from the back and wheeling it inside.

Adele opened the door to the room and handed the key to her mother with some reluctance.

"Thank you." Lani's voice cracked and her eyes welled with fresh tears. "Both of you."

"Come on, Dellie." Pop patted Adele's shoulder. "Let's give your mother a chance to get settled. Dinner starts at six," he told Lani. "If you want, after you eat, you can go to the kitchen and help the staff clean up. They're always shorthanded. Cook will tell you what to do."

Lani simply nodded and quickly shut the door behind them.

Her mother's hurry to be alone might be because she was going to start crying again, Adele thought, and her determination to remain unaffected battled with concern. Not caring was easier when Lani lived hundreds of miles away.

"She's in sorry shape," Pop said once they'd gotten back in the golf cart and were putt-putting down the road to the lodge.

"Is that why you agreed to let her stay on?"

"Partly."

"You're not usually such a softy. Especially where Mom's concerned."

In fact, the last time Lani had dropped Adele off at Seven Cedars, Pop had told Lani that Adele was staying with him for good and for her not to set foot on the place again. Adele had been fourteen at the time, but she remembered their huge fight as if it had been last week.

Lani had respected Pop's demand and never come back. Until today. Adele had finished out high school in Markton and then left for the University of Wyoming, seeing her mother only on occasion. When she'd returned to Seven Cedars after graduation, it had been like coming home.

"Maybe it's time to let bygones be bygones."

Adele wasn't so sure about that. There were too many bygones to let go of easily.

They reached the lodge, and she parked the golf cart under the same tree. Pop started to get out, but she stopped him with a hand on his arm.

"Considering the way Mom's always treated you, you have no reason to show her the tiniest kindness, much less forgiveness."

Pop sighed, removed an unused toothpick from his front shirt pocket and stuck it in his mouth. "Your mom's made a lot of mistakes in her life, but she did one thing right. For which I'm very grateful."

"What's that?"

"She gave me and your grandmother legal

guardianship of you back when you were fifteen. She didn't have to do that."

"She gave you guardianship?" Adele's jaw went slack.

"Your dad signed off, too."

"Why didn't you tell me?"

"Lani didn't want you to think your parents had abandoned you."

"But they did," Adele insisted. A year after that dreadful day and terrible fight.

"Depends, I guess, on how you look at it. They weren't such bad parents that they didn't realize you needed a real home and someone to take care of you."

With that, her grandfather left Adele sitting alone in the golf cart, reeling from her second shock that day.

All this time, she'd believed her grandparents had wanted her. Had fought to have her.

Instead, her mother and father had simply handed her over, like an old set of golf clubs or a broken TV.

Worse, none of them, not even Pop, had had the decency to tell her.

A wall of chilly air greeted Ty the moment he stepped outside his cabin. For a moment he considered driving to the barn, then decided a brisk walk would jump-start his sluggish system.

Normally an early riser, he was up and at it even earlier than usual thanks to a restless night. The reason for his tossing and turning was the same as his trip to the barn at half past the crack of dawn. Hamm hadn't been himself yesterday and appeared to be favoring his right front leg. After having his other horse suffer a debilitating injury, Ty was cautious when it came to Hamm. Some might say overly cautious.

In his mind, he had good reason. He couldn't afford another setback. Not this far into the rodeo season.

He briefly considered stopping at the dining hall and grabbing a cup of coffee. They weren't scheduled to start serving for another twenty minutes, but as Stick had promised on Ty's first day, Cook was very accommodating to the guests. Ty's concern for Hamm took precedence, however, and he made straight for the main barn.

The ranch hands had just begun feeding when he got there. While Hamm was happy to see him, he was more interested in breakfast. The big horse paced back and forth in anticipation as the feed wagon moved slowly down the aisle. Ty used the opportunity to observe the worrisome front leg.

Hamm grabbed a bite of hay even before the thick flake was dropped into his feed trough. He then ignored the hay in favor of the grain that followed, snorting lustily.

Now that he was standing still, Ty entered the stall and ran his hand over Hamm's front leg, paying particular attention to the knee area. It looked normal. No swelling or bruising. Next, he hefted Hamm's foot and, using a penknife, checked under the shoe. Hamm didn't so much as blink during the entire examination. Could be because he was fine. Could be because he was too busy eating to care about a little tenderness.

After another minute and a pat to Hamm's rump, Ty decided to get that cup of coffee in the dining hall and come back when the horse had finished eating. Then he'd take him to the round pen, work him a few minutes and get a better look at the leg, just to be one hundred percent sure.

Maybe he'd ask Adele to join him and give an opinion. She had a good eye when it came to both riders and their horses. It also gave him an excuse to see her. She'd missed dinner the previous evening. He assumed whatever work she'd mentioned at lunch with Garth and Reese must have kept her busy.

In the dining hall, the aroma of breakfast proved too tempting to resist. When one of the waitstaff brought out a tray of freshly baked cinnamon rolls, two somehow made it onto Ty's plate before he realized it. He no sooner sat down to eat then he noticed Adele cutting across the large and noisy room toward the kitchen.

Her gaze didn't waver from the floor in front of her, which was certainly strange. She was often in a hurry, especially in the mornings. But she always had a wave or smile for the guests. Ty's curiosity lasted only until she disappeared behind the kitchen's double doors and he took his first bite of the warm and gooey cinnamon roll.

Thirty minutes and one full stomach later, Ty was back in the barn. Haltering Hamm, he led the horse to the round pen. There, he put him through his paces, mostly satisfied that whatever had been bothering him yesterday, if anything, was no longer an issue. Nonetheless, he'd watch Hamm closely during morning class.

After walking him several times around all three barns to cool him down, Ty returned the horse to his stall. Class didn't start until nine, leaving a good hour to kill. Not really enough time to go back to his cabin. Ty supposed he could grab another cup of coffee in the dining hall.

It was then he saw Adele heading into the small barn where she and Pop kept their private stock. Even at a distance, she still appeared distracted. Then it hit Ty. Her mare—Crackers?—was due to deliver any day. That could explain Adele's unusual behavior, especially if there was a problem with the birth.

On impulse, Ty followed her into the barn and, as he'd guessed, found her at Crackers's stall. She had her arms resting on the door and was staring, unseeing, at the mare and newborn foal standing by her side.

"She had the baby," Ty said, approaching quietly.

Adele started at the sight of him but recovered quickly. "Sometime last night. A filly."

The foal, initially wary, relaxed enough around her human visitors to begin nursing. Ty noticed she stood straight and that her weight was good. A blanket of white spots covered her hind end. "She looks healthy."

"Seems to be. The vet is coming out later this morning to check on her."

"Nice markings, too. Going to be an Appaloosa like the mare."

For the first time that morning Adele looked Ty fully in the face. He was momentarily taken aback by the dark smudges beneath her eyes. She hadn't slept well, either.

"Are you okay?" The question slipped out automatically.

"I'm fine." She tried to smile, but it was lopsided. Then it wobbled.

"Adele."

All at once, she let out a sob. Her attempts to swallow a second one failed.

Ty responded without thinking. Reaching for her, he pulled her into his arms.

Her immediate response was to stiffen and draw back, as if she suddenly realized what she'd done.

"It's okay," he murmured, and she relented, burying her face in his shirt.

"I'm sorry."

"Don't be." He patted her back.

Normally, Ty avoided crying women, or at least kept his distance. Like a lot of his male brethren, he supposed, he didn't know what to say or how to act. His confusion was ten times worse if he was the cause of the woman's distress.

For some reason, it felt different with Adele. And not just because he was relatively certain someone else was responsible for her being upset.

He guessed she didn't often let down her guard. That she did so in front of him, allowed him to offer her comfort, showed just how much she trusted him and—was it possible?—liked him.

Tilting her head back, she looked up at him, blinking back the last of her tears. "I can't imagine what you think of me." Her damp lashes had formed tiny spikes that surrounded her liquid green eyes.

Ty was captivated. Driven by a force he couldn't resist, he lowered his head and pressed his mouth to hers.

Just one taste. One tiny sip of her petal-soft lips. He wanted more. Any man in his right mind would. But even this infinitesimal piece of heaven was more than he was entitled to. Whatever upset Adele had left her vulnerable, and he wasn't one to take advantage of that.

With a last featherlight brush of his lips against hers, he drew back—only to have Adele stop him with a tug on his jacket.

Clutching the thick fabric in her hands, she drew him closer.

Clearly, her emotions had gotten the better of her, and she wasn't thinking straight. If Ty were a gentleman, he'd tactfully disengage himself from her embrace. At the first touch of her tongue to his, however, *his* emotions got the better of *him*. When he heard Adele's soft moan and felt her arms circle his neck, he was a lost man.

The longer their kiss lasted, the more difficult it became for him to restrain himself. She felt exquisite, a maddening combination of taut muscles and soft curves. She tasted even better, like biting into another one of those freshly baked cinnamon rolls.

Just when the last of his restraint threatened to snap, she broke off their kiss, stepped back and placed her palms on his chest. Both of them were breathing hard. Her tears, he noted, had dried.

"Adele."

She shook her head and shushed him with a finger to her lips.

He hoped she wasn't planning on apologizing, because he sure wasn't sorry about what had happened. No way.

"If you're—"

She silenced him with another head shake, and cut her eyes to a place just over his shoulder.

All at once the hairs on Ty's neck rose, and he sensed they weren't alone.

"Shoot," he muttered.

"Yeah," Adele agreed.

A moment later Ty heard a loud voice say, "What in tarnation is going on here?"

He turned, expecting to see Pop.

What he didn't expect was the woman accompanying him, her face an older, harsher version of Adele's.

Grinning saucily, she gave Ty a thorough once-over. "Well, ain't you something."

Behind him, Adele softly swore.

"Is she your mother?"

"Yes."

"You look kind of alike."

Adele grumbled to herself. If Ty had so easily spotted the resemblance, so would everyone at the ranch.

"She here for a visit?"

"Sort of." After only two meals, dinner last night and breakfast this morning, Lani was fast becoming useful in the kitchen—a surprising turn of events that didn't make Adele one bit happy.

"How long is she staying?"

"Not long." *Better not be.*

"I'm sorry about putting you in a, ah, compromising situation back there," he said.

They were walking toward the main arena, though walking was a loose term. Adele was practically running, and Ty, even with his six-foot-plus height, was forced to take long strides in order to keep up with her. She didn't want him accompanying her, but after getting caught kissing him, by her grandfather and mother, it didn't seem fair or right telling him to beat it.

"You weren't the only one participating in…what happened."

He chuckled. "For which I'm damn glad."

"I shouldn't have—" She swallowed to clear the lump in her throat. Allowing her emotions to run amok was what had landed her in this jam in the first place. Why had her mother chosen now to show up? Why had she shown up at all? And why did Ty have to be such a good kisser? "I shouldn't have allowed things to go as far as they did."

"What now?" There was a hint of amusement in his voice. "Are we going to pretend we didn't kiss?"

Adele would like nothing better. However, she was relatively certain she'd remember kissing Ty for the rest of her life. In vivid detail.

"I think we should try."

He laughed out loud.

She frowned and trudged ahead.

They reached the main arena and went in through the gate. Beginner class was scheduled to start soon. Some of the students were already warming up their horses in the adjoining, smaller arena.

Ty followed Adele to the holding pen that housed the calves, and busied himself checking on the gate while she reviewed a list of instructions with the wrangler. When they were done, she made an effort to shake Ty by suggesting, "Go ahead and saddle up if you want. Class starts soon."

"What about your horse?"

"Stick's supposed to be taking care of that for me." Fingers crossed, the kid was doing his job. Adele dreaded going into the barn, just in case Pop and her mother were still there.

And speaking of Pop and her mother, just

what the heck were they doing together? In her embarrassment and haste to get away, Adele had forgotten to ask. Anybody else and she'd have believed they were wanting a peek at the new filly. But Pop and Lani didn't take strolls around the ranch together.

As soon as class was over, she intended to find her grandfather and pester him until she got an answer.

But before then, she was going to have to relieve herself of Ty's company. Covering the last item on her list with the wrangler, she left him to join Ty at the gate. Subtleties hadn't worked, so she tried being direct.

"You need to leave now," she told him. "To get ready."

"I will leave." He flashed her that killer sexy grin again. "As soon as you agree to meet me after class. We need to talk."

She cast a furtive glance at the wrangler, who appeared to be occupied with his task of separating the calves, but was probably hanging on their every word. "I thought we agreed to pretend that didn't happen," she hissed.

"I meant about your mother."

She drew back, completely caught off guard. "Hell no."

His grin widened. "You owe me that much.

For allowing things to go as far as they did," he said, quoting her.

"You started it."

"I admit, I'm a man and a pushover when it comes to a crying woman."

She glanced over her shoulder at the wrangler and grimaced. How long until this piece of juicy gossip made the rounds of the ranch?

She conceded to Ty's request only to get rid of him. "I'll meet you in the barn office at eleven-thirty."

"I have a better idea."

She didn't like the glint in his eyes.

"Take me on a tour of the ranch."

"A tour?"

"Our horses will already be saddled. And I've been wanting to see the place since I arrived."

"Fine," Adele reluctantly agreed.

She just wished part of her wasn't thrilled and eagerly anticipating a ride with him.

Chapter 5

Ty collected Hamm from where he'd left him tethered in the barn. Tired of standing, the horse practically knocked Ty over in his haste to get outside. Ty didn't mind. He admired the horse's natural athleticism and endless energy. If they could just get in sync like him and his last horse, they'd be unbeatable.

A quick stop at the water trough proved to be a waste of time. Hamm wasn't interested in drinking. He did no more than splash water with his snout, reminding Ty of that old saying about leading a horse to water.

Adele hadn't specified a meeting place, so Ty led Hamm toward the open area in front of the barns, figuring he'd see her eventually. He ran into two of his classmates near the smaller practice arena—Mike and his wife, the woman who talked a lot during class. Thankfully, her name came to Ty a split second before she hailed him.

"Hey there, Ty."

"How you doing, Sandy? Mike? Getting some extra practice in?"

The couple was taking turns tossing ropes at a stationary practice dummy.

"Yeah." Mike grinned sheepishly. "I can't quite figure out what Adele was trying to show us this morning." He wound his rope into a loose coil.

Sandy laughed. "I can't figure out *any* of it. But it's still a hoot." Of the two of them, she was the less serious and the less coordinated. That didn't stop her from enjoying herself, a trait Ty admired.

He wondered what it would be like to have the kind of affectionate and supportive relationship Mike and Sandy did. He met a lot of women on the rodeo circuit, but most were either competitors focused on their own careers or buckle bunnies with a personal agenda that didn't appeal to Ty.

Like Adele's mother.

He hadn't said anything to Adele, but he'd recognized Lani the moment he saw her. No surprise, really. Rodeo folk might be spread from one corner of the globe to the other, but they were also a small community unto themselves. Everybody knew everybody, or at least had heard of them. Lani had been a member of the rodeo world far too long for Ty not to have run into her now and again through the years.

He was no authority on reading people, but he'd wager Adele wasn't close to her, judging from the look she'd given Lani earlier.

"You think you could watch me throw a few and see what I'm doing wrong?" Mike asked.

"If you don't mind," Sandy hurriedly added. "We don't want to keep you."

"Sure. Why not?" Ty was early and Adele was nowhere in sight. "I can spare a few minutes."

"Taking a ride?" The woman's attention strayed to Hamm, who was pawing the ground impatiently.

"Thinking about it."

They didn't need to know he was touring the ranch with Adele. And if she failed to show up as promised…well, he could always ride around the ranch by himself.

Tethering Hamm to a nearby post, he perused the open area one last time. No Adele.

"Go ahead." Ty turned his attention to Mike. "Show me what you've got."

The man raised his arm over his head and swung his rope in a circle before tossing it at the fake cow head. The lasso just missed.

"Dang." Mike shook his head in disgust. "I think I might need glasses."

"Do it again." Ty studied him closely while he repeated the exercise, and came to the same conclusion he had the first time. "This time, try shifting your weight just slightly to your left foot."

Mike did and his next toss landed where it should, if a little lopsided.

"All right!" He beamed.

"One more time."

Mike threw the rope again with the same results.

"Good job." Sandy clapped.

"Can you feel the difference?" Ty asked.

"Yeah." Mike rolled his right shoulder as if testing it.

"Your center of gravity was off."

He laughed and shook his head. "Sounds too simple."

Ty didn't comment. He was too busy replaying his statement to Mike over and over in his head.

Center of gravity. He should have picked up on that in the beginners' class, when Adele had had him riding with his eyes closed. He'd repeated the exercise several times since, until he felt he knew which way Hamm would turn even before the horse did. But Ty hadn't paid attention to his center of gravity while throwing the rope.

Another point-two second gain in his time was staring him smack in the face.

What was wrong with him that he hadn't seen these mistakes before? He was hardly a novice. Blaming four years of competing exclusively on one horse was beginning to sound like a lame excuse. In reality, Ty's inflated ego and overabundance of confidence had gotten in the way, convincing him he needed to retrain Hamm rather than retrain himself.

While Ty was absorbed with this latest revelation, two things happened. Mike continued to throw more successful tosses and Adele emerged from the barn astride the paint mare she'd usually rode.

"Hey, I've got to go," he told Mike and Sandy.

"See you at dinner?" Hope shone in Sandy's eyes.

"You bet."

"Thanks for your help." Mike extended his hand, and Ty shook it.

"My pleasure."

And it was. Ty had enjoyed giving Mike pointers. On top of that, he'd learned something valuable about himself.

From the corner of his eye he spotted Adele riding in his direction. Memories of their kiss returned, and he forgot all about Mike and Sandy and roping and pretty much everything else except her.

Riding to meet her halfway, he ignored the stares of nearby wranglers. He couldn't be the first guest Adele had taken on a tour.

"Where would you like to start?" she asked, as Hamm tried to make friends with the mare by stretching his head out and sniffing her. The mare responded by pinning her ears back and playing hard to get.

"How far is Little Twister Creek?" Other than that one afternoon in Markton, and walking to and from his cabin, Ty had seen almost nothing of the countryside.

"A few miles. More than we can fit in this afternoon."

"Then how 'bout just around the ranch?"

She took him through three gates. At each one, she opened the latch and swung the gate wide without dismounting. When they were both through, she pushed it shut and relatched it, also without dismounting.

"You've been working with her," Ty said as they rode across the big pasture.

"Bella can be a bit flighty, but she's learning." Adele nudged the mare into a slow trot, but not before he glimpsed her eyes warming with pleasure at his compliment.

"How long have you had her?"

"A month or so. I'm training her for a client."

"You do that often?"

"Sometimes. Depends on the horse and the client."

With Adele riding in front, they picked their way along a winding trail toward a man-made stock pond.

"Did your grandfather raise cattle long?"

"A lot of years. He bought Seven Cedars back in the sixties after he retired from rodeoing. The ranch isn't as large as some of the other ones in the area, but he did pretty well until about eight years ago."

"What happened? The economy?"

Adele hesitated briefly before answering. "My grandmother died."

"I'm sorry."

"It was hard on Pop."

It had been hard on Adele, too. Ty could tell. "When did he lose his thumb?"

"Oh, gosh, over forty years ago. That was the reason he quit rodeoing."

"A roping accident?"

"Yeah. His thumb got twisted in the rope. The horse went one way and the calf another."

"Some guys still compete without a thumb." The loss of a digit wasn't entirely uncommon with ropers.

"Pop says he was ready to retire, anyway."

"Well, this is a nice place to retire to."

Winged insects, buzzing in the warm midday sun, flitted over the pond's glassy surface, dipping occasionally to take a sip of moisture. Suddenly, there was a small splash in the center of the pond. Ty had the urge to bring his rod and reel another day and go after one of those bass making a meal of the flying insects.

"So, when did you come here to live?"

"I visited Pop off and on ever since I was a kid. We didn't start Cowboy College until after I earned my business degree." More hesitancy before answering. Whatever else there was to the story, she wasn't saying.

They'd passed the pond and were now on a slightly wider trail that allowed Ty and Adele to ride side by side. The arrangement also pleased Hamm, who continued trying to win Bella over with little love nips. Unfortunately for him, she remained indifferent.

"I like what I do." Adele gave Ty a shy smile. Her eyes, however, were lit up, their brilliance captivating him. "Technically, it's work, but most days it feels a whole lot more like playing."

"Can't blame you. This is a great place to work. Wish I'd thought of opening a roping school."

"We're a little remote for some people."

"That's what makes it so nice. I could see myself living here." His gaze traveled to the distant mountains, their tops peeking through a blanket of wispy white clouds.

"Not some big fancy ranch?"

"If you're referring to your neighbors, no." He gave her a wry smile. "Though I admit I wouldn't mind heading over to Garth's place one day just to check it out." His grin widened. "Maybe you can take me."

"We'll see." Her expression instantly closed.

Had he pushed her too far, reminding her of their kiss earlier? He wanted to talk about it, but gut instinct told him she wasn't ready.

After several minutes of riding in silence, Ty asked, "Do you have any other family in the area?"

"You mean besides my mother?"

He didn't react to the bitterness in Adele's voice. "Here or anywhere."

"My dad's in Lubbock, Texas. He moved there about fifteen years ago after marrying my stepmom."

"Did your dad rodeo, too?"

"For a while. He quit when I was young."

The careful answers Adele delivered told Ty more about her and her childhood than the sparse and rehearsed information she provided.

"Do you see much of them?"

"No," she answered, with a finality that implied the subject was closed.

He took the hint and gave her some space.

"I read somewhere you're from Santa Fe," she said after a few minutes. "Is your family still there?"

"Most of them. A few years ago my folks

sold their place and bought a smaller one closer to town."

"Were they rodeo people, too?"

"No. Dad's a mortgage broker and Mom's a real estate agent. They've always ridden, so we had horses growing up."

"How did you start rodeoing?"

"Friends. I got serious in high school. About that and football. I had trouble deciding between the two after graduation."

"What made you pick rodeoing?"

"I won All Around Cowboy at the National High School Finals Rodeo my senior year. I was hooked after that. Luckily, my family's supported me or I wouldn't have made it. Financially or emotionally."

Rodeoing wasn't cheap, and until he'd started winning, Ty, like a lot of competitors, had depended on his family to supplement his income.

"Losing the Iron Grip Ropes sponsorship cost me more than a career opportunity," he continued. "I was counting on the money that came with it to pay back my parents."

"Does your younger sister rodeo?" Adele asked. "You said she wanted to learn to rope."

"She tried barrel racing for a while, but

didn't stick with it. My older sister's a single mom with two little girls."

"That must be rough."

"She's doing okay. She has her real estate license and works with our mom. I keep a fifth-wheel trailer at her place and stay there when I'm not traveling. The rent helps. She and my mom have been struggling these last couple years, what with the real estate market being so up and down. Mom's worried about keeping the business afloat. And Dad's job is just crazy. Changing every day."

"I bet."

Ty pushed down on his right stirrup, adjusted his saddle, which had shifted slightly, and said determinedly, "Another reason I don't intend to lose the championship a second time."

"Is your little sister coming out?" Adele asked.

"She'd like to, but probably not. Right now, she's doing an internship with a large animal surgery center."

"She's a vet?"

"Officially, not until next month, when she graduates school." A wave of nostalgia struck Ty, and he made a mental note to call his family tonight.

"Hey, check that out." Adele reined in her

mare and pointed to a cluster of trees. Behind the grove, the land sloped down into a small draw. "Is that what I think it is?"

Ty stopped beside her and peered into the trees. He immediately spotted the small face staring at them from between low hanging branches. "One of yours?"

"Has to be. Two head went missing a couple weeks ago, when they got through a hole in the fence during the night. I figured they'd gotten lost or…" She grimaced.

"At least one of them has escaped being a meal."

"You game?" Challenge glinted in her green eyes.

"Are you kidding? I'm always game."

They both untied their lassos from their saddles. The calf, about forty yards away, observed them warily.

All at once Adele shouted, "Go," and the chase was on.

Adele pressed her legs into Bella's flanks. The mare immediately went from a standstill to a full gallop. With Ty right beside her, they bore down on the lone calf. Because Bella was smaller and quicker than Hamm, Adele took the header position. Ty remained a length behind, in the heeler position. Team roping wasn't her specialty, but she'd done enough of it through the years to hold her own, even with someone of Ty's caliber.

Considering they were unaccustomed to roping as a team, they worked well together, automatically anticipating and compensating for each other's moves. The calf, spooked into action, had spun sideways and was hightailing it through the trees as fast as his stubby legs could carry him. He headed toward the narrow draw, bawling loudly, then dropped out of sight beneath the rim. Adele and Ty bent low on their horses' necks and flew down the side of the draw.

An exuberant "Yee-haw" erupted from her throat before she even realized it, then "Come on, Bella," when the calf unexpectedly cut to the right.

Her mare's front hooves hit the ground at the base of the draw like a ton of bricks. Adele hung on, the resulting jar to her system acting like a shot of adrenaline. A quick glance over her shoulder assured her Ty was having no trouble keeping up. Pure unabashed joy lit his face. Her own jaw hurt from smiling so hard.

Chunks of dirt exploded from beneath their horses' hooves as they gained ground on the tiring calf. In the next few seconds, they closed the distance to mere feet. Sensing the moment was right, they reached for their lassos. Adele threw hers at the calf's head a heartbeat ahead of Ty. He aimed his for the animal's rear feet. Her lasso landed where it should, around the horns. Ty's didn't, falling instead to the ground.

The calf jumped and twisted, shaking his head and fighting to break free. Adele reined Bella to a stop and backed her up to bring the line taut. Ty collected his rope and wound it into a coil, a sour expression on his face. He obviously didn't like missing his throws.

Giving their heavily breathing horses a rest, they dismounted. By then, the calf stood quietly, nostrils flaring and flanks heaving, resigned to the fact that his wandering days were at an end.

"Don't look so miserable, buddy." Adele removed her rope, wrapped it around the calf's neck and tied a knot, one designed for safely leading him back home. "We just saved your life. With all the wolves, bears and mountain lions in this area, I can't believe you've survived this long."

Feeling Ty's gaze on her, she looked up, momentarily stuck by what she was doing here with him. She didn't act spontaneously.

She certainly didn't tear across the countryside chasing down calves with men she hardly knew. On a bet, for crying out loud.

She didn't normally kiss them, either, but she'd done all those things with Ty, in the same day, no less.

When he didn't say anything, she asked, "What?"

"You look happy."

"That was fun." Okay, she'd confessed, and the ground hadn't opened up to swallow her whole.

"You should do it more often."

"Catch stray calves?" She laughed.

"Have fun. And laugh." His brown eyes bored into hers, studying but not judging. "I'm thinking you don't do either enough."

According to her grandfather, she also didn't date enough. Had she really become that much of a stick-in-the-mud? And when had it happened? Adele didn't like the momentary glimpse of herself through another's eyes.

"Sorry about missing earlier," he said with what might have been embarrassment.

"I doubt that happens much with you."

"No. And I'm not sure why it happened now."

"Mind if I make an observation?"

"That's why I came here."

"Hamm takes aim with his right eye."

"He does?" Ty pushed back his cowboy hat, scratched his head. "I must have watched a half-dozen films of myself on Hamm, and I never noticed."

"You might not if you weren't looking."

He closed his eyes, his brow furrowed in concentration. Adele imagined he was mentally replaying his run, feeling the barely noticeable tug on the reins as Hamm turned his head to the left in order to see better. Realizing he should be loosening the reins and shifting his weight.

"You're right." He opened his eyes and grinned. "You can spot me any day."

Pleasure coursed through her. Satisfaction at helping a student improve—that was her job, after all. But something else. Something having to do entirely with Ty.

"We'd better get this little fellow back home," she said, to cover her sudden rush of emotions. Leading the calf behind her, she mounted Bella and dallied the rope around her saddle horn, glad to be returning home. Ty had an infuriating way of unsettling her.

He also mounted. "Maybe we can finish our tour of the ranch tomorrow."

Of course he would remember.

"We'll see."

Adele clucked to Bella, who obediently began walking out. Ty fell in step beside her, and the calf brought up the rear, not liking the rope, but having no choice in the matter. Soon enough, he settled down.

Their slow climb up and out of the draw wasn't nearly as thrilling as galloping down into it had been.

At the top, Adele pointed to a trail. "This one circles back around to the east pasture."

They slowed their pace to accommodate the calf's exhausted state and recalcitrant nature.

"What made your grandfather pick this place?" As they meandered along, he took in the rolling green landscape and startling blue skies.

"Pop was friends with Garth's grandfather. He told Pop about the vacant land bordering his ranch being for sale. Pop and my grandmother had visited a few times and liked the area. They wound up buying the land sight unseen."

"My mother would never recommend that to a client, but in your grandfather's case, he made a wise decision."

"He and my grandmother lived in a camper

for six months while the original ranch house was being constructed. The crew barely finished before the first snow hit. Lucky for Pop, because Grandma might have left him otherwise."

"Can't say I'd have blamed her. It must get pretty cold here in winter."

"Twenty degrees on a warm day. But it's really pretty in a primitive way."

"I'd like to see that."

"There's some good skiing up north."

"I was thinking more along the lines of sitting in front of a roaring fire." Ty's eyes locked with hers. "Snuggled under a blanket."

"Oh." Adele required several seconds and a fair amount of throat clearing to recover. "Pop, um, built the stock barn and the main arena the following spring."

Ty didn't resist her efforts to return the conversation to their earlier topic. Thank goodness.

"When did you start Cowboy College?"

"About seven years ago. We began with the main lodge and the inn building. The cabins came later, a few each year as we grew."

"That was quite a risk you took."

"Pop's the one who took the risk. He invested his life's savings in Cowboy College. And it's paid off."

"You've worked hard." Ty sent her an admiring glance.

Adele waited for the wariness that usually overcame her when a man showed signs of interest. Only it didn't happen, and she couldn't help wondering why. Ty was a poor choice for any romantic entanglements, short-term or long. She should be doubly cautious.

Then it occurred to her that maybe his leaving soon was the reason she felt less on guard. No way would she be stupid enough to let herself fall for him, only to be hurt later. She was too smart for that. Too careful. Knowing she'd keep her heart under lock and key allowed her to let loose a little. Laugh. Chase calves.

Because he was…safe.

She relaxed, her newfound discovery giving her confidence—until he looked at her with a much too endearing expression on his handsome face.

"Do you like to fish?"

"I used to. Pop would take me sometimes when I was young."

"You want to go one day? I hear the fly-fishing's pretty good at Little Twister Creek."

"I, ah…" Feeling safe with Ty—make that *semi*safe—didn't mean she was ready for a date. "We're so busy right now, I really can't afford the time off."

"Well, if you wind up with a free morning or afternoon, let me know. The invitation's always open."

For just a moment, she indulged her imagination and pictured the two of them whiling away a lazy afternoon on the banks of Little Twister Creek. It could be—here was that word again—*fun*.

The discussion changed to roping and the upcoming Buffalo Bill Cody Stampede Rodeo. Ty gave his opinion on who he considered his toughest competition, which included her neighbor, Garth Maitland.

"Will you come watch?" he asked.

"I wouldn't miss it. We usually take a group of students along, too."

They reached the first gate, and once again, Adele opened it without dismounting. When she went to close it, Ty stopped her.

"Can I try?"

"Sure." She backed Bella up to give him and Hamm room. When he succeeded in closing the gate with no problem, Adele tipped her head appreciatively. "Nicely done."

"We're learning to work together, too."

The calf abruptly let out a noisy bawl.

"Guess he's glad to be home." She started forward. This time the animal followed willingly, in a hurry to be reunited with his pals crowding together at the fence in order to get a look at him.

"He's not the only eager one." Ty had to hold Hamm back from running a race to the barn.

They rode first to the calf pen and dropped off their charge in the care of the assistant stock manager, then walked their horses to the barns. When they reached the place where they would separate—he was going to the main barn, she to the smaller one—they stopped as if on cue.

"Thanks for the tour," he said, with that sexy half smile she'd seen countless times in magazines, on cable television and the big screen at rodeos. Only this time, the smile was directed at her. "I know I kind of tricked you into it."

"Kind of?"

"But if we hadn't gone, we wouldn't have found the calf, and you wouldn't have shown me how Hamm takes aim."

Or had such a good time team roping, she thought.

"I might have shown you. Eventually," she said with a grin, and quickly escaped to the quiet seclusion of the barn, where she could give her wildly beating heart a chance to slow.

Who was she fooling, thinking Ty Boudeau was safe? He was as dangerous as they came, especially to someone like her, a country girl with little experience around men like him.

Just as Adele was latching the door to Bella's stall, a woman's voice sounded from behind her.

"That's one fine looking cowboy."

Her mother, of course, would notice, having made fine looking cowboys the focus of her entire adult life. Still, Adele couldn't disagree.

"I suppose."

"He likes you." Lani accompanied Adele to the tack room in the center of the barn, where she hung the mare's bridle on a peg. "You like him, too."

"He's a student, Mom." Adele bristled, the remark hitting too close to home. "And a guest of the ranch. That's all."

She walked away, well aware that her reaction was over the top. But hell would freeze over before she'd discuss Ty with her mother.

"Wait," Lani called after her, struggling a little to catch up, her breathing shallow and raspy.

Smoking and hard living did that to a person. Only now that Adele thought about it, she hadn't seen her mother with a cigarette or a drink since she'd arrived. Knowing her, she'd probably gotten better at hiding her vices.

"You have every right to be mad at me," Lani said.

The admission was the last thing Adele had expected to issue from her mother's lips. Ever. It brought her to a standstill.

"I have to get to the office," she said, fighting an unwelcome rush of emotion. "Some new guests are arriving this afternoon."

"I'd really like to talk to you."

Adele inched away. "Not now."

"You can't keep avoiding me."

"Why not, Mom?" She spun around. "You avoided me for years."

"I guess I deserve that."

Whatever else Lani intended to say was cut short by Stick barreling down the barn aisle toward them, his shirttail flying and his freckled face flushed beet-red from exertion.

"Adele, Adele! Come quick."

"What's wrong?" she asked, alarmed by the sight of him.

"It's Pop," he said, holding his sides. "He fell. And he's hurt bad."

Chapter 6

Adele reached her grandfather first, ahead of Stick and her mother. He lay flat on his back on the muddy ground near the water trough. Ty, of all people, was kneeling beside him. Where had he come from and how did he get there ahead of her?

"Pop, are you okay?" Breathless from running, Adele bent at the waist and braced her hands on her thighs.

"I'll live," he muttered, his chest rising and falling.

"You're lucky you didn't crack your head open on the trough."

Pop groaned when Ty lifted him to a sitting position.

"Careful," she warned. "He may have broken something." She thought of Pop's hip, the one that was always giving him trouble.

"Quit being such a mother hen."

She ignored her grandfather's comment and came closer, intent on verifying for herself his claim of being uninjured. "What happened?"

"That damn spigot's been leaking for days. Figured I'd fix it." His face twisted into a painful grimace when Ty stood and hauled him to his feet. Putting out a hand in protest, Pop said, "Give me a minute, would you?" in a strained voice.

"Sorry." Ty relaxed his grip but didn't let go. Good thing, because Pop swayed unsteadily.

"Maybe we shouldn't have moved him just yet." Adele hovered, the mud her grandfather had slipped in pulling at her boots and sucking her in. It also covered her grandfather from head to toe, probably soaking through his clothes.

Several more guests and the assistant barn manager had come over to investigate, crowding around them. Their anxious chatter and proximity grated on Adele's already frayed nerves.

"Can everyone step back, please. He needs room."

"Don't mind her," Pop told Ty. "The least little thing sets her in a tizzy."

"This is hardly the least little thing," she retorted hotly. "You're hurt."

"I'm fine."

"Can you walk?"

"I'm getting to it."

Distressed by the sight of her grandfather's ashen complexion and his attempts to dismiss what could be a serious injury, she confronted Stick. "Why didn't you help him when he fell?"

"Ty got there first. Pop didn't want to tell you, but Ty—"

"You weren't going to tell me?" Adele demanded of her grandfather.

He shot her an isn't-it-obvious-why look. "Don't know what all the fuss is about. I just had the wind knocked out of me."

"And now you can hardly stand, much less walk."

"The hell I can't walk." He shook off Ty's hold.

Adele watched, biting her lower lip. To her relief, Pop didn't topple, but neither did he attempt to take a step. She sent Ty a worried glance behind her grandfather's back.

He nodded reassuringly, letting her know he wasn't moving from Pop's side.

The seconds dragged by. Finally, Pop attempted a step—and his knees went right out from under him. Ty easily caught him when he pitched forward. Thank goodness.

Adele panicked at the sight of her grandfather's pale face. "I think we should call 911."

"You'll do no such thing."

"You need to see a doctor. You could have broken a rib or sprained an ankle."

He made a sound of disgust.

"She has a point," Ty said.

"That's enough out of the both of you."

"I have an idea." Adele turned to Stick. "Find Mike Scolari and bring him here. His cabin number is fourteen. If he's not there, go to the office and have Gayle pull up his reservation record. His cell phone will be listed under guest information."

"Mike? The husband of Sandy, who talks nonstop?" Ty asked.

"Yes." Adele nodded, her attention remaining on her grandfather.

"What can he do?"

"Mike's a doctor."

"You're kidding!"

"I don't need a doctor," Pop groused.

"Yes, you do," Adele insisted. To Stick, she said, "Hurry."

"Take one step and you're fired."

Stick's gaze traveled between Adele and her grandfather. "Sorry, Pop," he said, and dashed off to do her bidding.

Smart kid.

"What's the matter with you?" she asked Ty, who continued to gape at her.

"I just can't believe Mike's a doctor."

"Because his wife talks a lot?"

"Because roping is a dangerous sport. I can't believe he'd risk injuring his hands."

"Mike's a pediatrician."

Wrong thing to say.

Pop exploded. "I ain't letting no kiddie doctor examine me."

"Then I'm taking you to the emergency room."

"The hell you are."

"Pop, please." She couldn't help the sob that infected her voice.

To her amazement, he conceded. "All right, all right."

"Mom." Adele reached into her jeans

pocket and fished out her keys. "Can you pull my truck around?"

"Of course, sweetie." Lani hurried off. A few minutes later, she returned in the truck.

After arranging a horse blanket on the front seat to protect it from all the mud, Ty helped Pop climb in. It was a struggle for both of them.

"Thank you, Ty," Adele said softly when they were done.

"I'll ride with you, just in case he needs help getting out."

She didn't want him along, but knowing her grandfather, he'd be more cooperative with Ty than her. "Okay."

He opened the rear passenger door and climbed in.

"I'll come, too," Lani said, and before Adele could stop her, she'd hopped in the rear driver's-side seat.

"Great." Adele's next thought vanished with the ringing of her cell phone. She recognized the number and quickly flipped the phone open. "Stick, did you find Mike?"

"Sure did."

"Meet us at Pop's house." She slid in behind the steering wheel and reached for her seat belt. "We're on our way."

* * *

Pop's house bore little resemblance to the modest structure he'd built over forty-five years earlier. Along with a room added on the back for Adele when she was eight, he'd constructed a new master bedroom suite and completely remodeled the downstairs, including the kitchen. Soon after his wife's death, however, he'd moved back into their old bedroom, and as far as Adele knew, no one had slept in the master bedroom since.

"Down the hall," she instructed Ty as soon as they entered the house. "Second door on the right."

"The family-room couch will do just fine," Pop grumbled.

"You need to lie down."

"What I need is a less bossy granddaughter."

Ty, his strong arm supporting Pop, changed direction, away from the hall and toward the family room.

"Hey!" Adele chased after them. "Ty," she pleaded when neither of them listened.

"It's his house," he said gently. "He has a right to go where he wants."

"I knew there was something I liked about

you." Pop grunted as Ty lowered him onto the leather couch. "You ain't afraid of her."

"Are you kidding?" Ty bent close to Pop's ear and whispered loudly, "I'm counting on you to protect me."

Pop laughed, and Adele breathed a sigh of relief. Maybe he wasn't badly hurt, after all.

Stick showed up with Mike Scolari. Adele wanted to stay with Pop during the examination, but he'd have none of it.

"Can't you give an old man some privacy?" he complained.

She and Ty joined her mother and Stick in the kitchen.

"A glass of water, anyone?" Lani asked.

She flitted around Pop's kitchen, making herself comfortable—which rankled Adele.

"No, thanks," she mumbled.

"I'll take one, if you don't mind." Stick accepted the tall glass Lani prepared for him, and guzzled it down.

"Your grandfather will be fine." Ty joined Adele at the table. The same table she had sat at whenever her mother dropped her off at Seven Cedars to stay. She'd been four the first time, and her feet hadn't touched the floor.

Seeing Lani standing by the sink unleashed an onslaught of memories Adele had been all too happy to shove to the back of her mind. For a moment, she became that little girl again, crying her heart out as she watched Lani's beat-up Mercury pull away from Pop's house and drive away.

Her mother had returned weeks—or was it months?—later. But she'd left Adele with her grandparents again the next year. Then again six months later. The pattern had been repeated with increasing frequency until Adele was fourteen. That summer, Lani and Pop got into a huge fight like never before, and Lani hadn't come back. From then on, the only time Adele saw her mother was during the holidays, when she flew out to wherever Lani was currently living, and only because her grandparents had insisted. Those visits stopped when Adele turned eighteen. After that, Adele saw Lani only when their paths happened to cross at some rodeo.

Looking back, she realized she hadn't visited her father any more than she had her mom. Her trips to Texas, at least, weren't strained, and peppered with petty outbursts. Her father had tried to include Adele in his life, which was more than she could say about Lani.

Mike entered the room, disrupting her thoughts. "You can see your grandfather now."

She stood, vaguely aware that Ty did, too. "How is he?"

"Tough as nails."

"Will he be all right?"

"I'm sure he's strained his back, though he won't admit it hurts."

Adele sighed.

"I gave him ibuprofen, triple the regular dose, told him to soak in a hot bath for an hour and to take it easy over the next couple of days."

She wondered how in the world she would manage that.

"I doubt anything's broken," Mike continued, "but I'd advise a trip to his regular doctor."

"Yeah." Yet another challenge to test her.

"I also offered him a lollipop, like I do my regular patients. He refused that, too."

"Are you making a joke?"

Mike chuckled and put a hand on Adele's shoulder. "He'll recover. Falls aren't uncommon with the elderly. Luckily, the ground was soft, and he didn't hit the water trough on his way down."

Elderly? Pop had always seemed ageless.

"If he has a bad night or appears worse in the morning, don't hesitate to call me."

Adele nodded. "Stick, take Dr. Scolari, Mr.

Boudeau and my mother back to their cabins, please."

"How 'bout I stay?" Ty offered in a soft voice. "Pop may need some help."

He might, even if it was just to undress for bed or get that hot soak in the tub. God knew Pop wouldn't accept Adele's assistance with those things.

"Okay."

"I want to stay, too, baby."

Her mother's show of concern was about two decades too late. "Don't you have to be at work?" Adele asked.

Lani's mouth compressed into a tight line, the reminder of her place at the ranch clearly stinging.

Adele didn't care. Pop was her top priority at the moment, and her mother wasn't anyone he wanted around.

More than that, *she* didn't want her mother around.

"Come on." Ty took Lani's elbow and gave her his most disarming smile. "I'll walk you to the truck."

She relented. Lani was always a sucker when it came to good-looking men.

Stick and Mike said their goodbyes, then followed Ty and Lani out the door. Adele didn't wait. She crossed the threshold into the family room before the kitchen door was closed.

Pop sat propped in a corner of the leather couch, his head tilted back, his eyes closed. She approached quietly, not wanting to disturb his sleep.

Only he wasn't sleeping, just resting, and he opened his eyes the instant she neared.

"I feel like a fool."

"You?" she chided, and perched gingerly on the opposite end of the couch to avoid causing his back discomfort. "A fool?"

"I suppose you think it was stupid of me to try and fix the spigot with all that mud."

"To be honest, I wouldn't have given it a second thought."

"I lost my balance, is all."

"Could've happened to anyone." She reached across the couch.

For several seconds he stared at her outstretched hand, then clasped it in his. Adele felt the world lift from her shoulders.

"Pop, can I ask you a question?"

"Sure."

"Why'd you agree to let Mom stay? And to give her a job?"

He raised his bushy silver eyebrows. "I told you, I think she's ready to make amends."

"I know. But when she left that summer I was fourteen, you told her to never come back."

"That's not entirely right."

His statement shocked Adele. "I was there. I heard the two of you fighting."

"You didn't hear everything." He expelled a long breath, readjusted his position and winced.

From pain or regret?

"What did I miss?"

His gaze turned inward. When he spoke, it was as if he was talking to Lani on that long-ago day. "I said 'if you ever come back, it had better be because you're ready to be a real mother to your daughter.'"

Adele remained quiet, not trusting her voice.

"The way I figure it," Pop continued, "if she finally got the nerve to face me, maybe she's finally ready to be that real mother to you."

If only Adele agreed with him.

Ty opened Pop's back door and stepped out onto the porch. In the distance, the sun was making another spectacular exit, sinking behind the mountains in a blaze of vivid reds and golds. What would it look like in winter, with snow covering those mountains and blanketing the land? Adele's earlier description tempted him to find out.

He wasn't usually one to notice nature's bounties, being too busy most of the time. It was different here at Seven Cedars. His frantic pace slowed enough for him to appreciate sunsets, and the smell of damp earth after a sudden shower, and the taste of freshly ground coffee enjoyed over a leisurely breakfast.

"How's he doing?" Adele rose from the rocker she'd been occupying.

He hadn't seen her sitting there, and tried to hide his delight. "Complaining up a storm."

"Complaining's good. It's when he doesn't that I really worry."

Ty held out the bottle of beer he'd carried with him. "Want a sip? Pop said to help myself."

"I don't usually drink beer." She took the bottle anyway and returned to her rocker.

Pulling up one of the empty stools, he sat beside her, the aged rattan seat creaking beneath his weight.

"Is he in bed?" Adele took a long swallow of Ty's beer.

He studied her every move. "Watching TV. Said no one had helped him take a bath since he was three, and he'd be damned before someone else does again."

"I'm sorry he was so uncooperative." She returned Ty's beer to him.

"No problem." He paused, studying the bottle in his hand, intensely aware of where her lips had been seconds before. Savoring the sense of anticipation for a tiny while longer, he finally put the bottle to his mouth and drained a third of its contents. "You really should call his doctor tomorrow."

Adele stopped rocking. "Is something wrong?"

"This isn't the first time he's fallen. He accidentally mentioned it during one of his grumblings. I thought you should know."

Frowning, she rubbed her forehead.

"Someone with his severe arthritis is bound to fall now and then," Ty said.

"I know. I just wish he wasn't so stubborn about getting hip replacement surgery."

"He wants to see you taken care of first."

Adele shot Ty a sideways look. "Did he tell you that?"

"He didn't have to. I can see it plain as day."

"This is ridiculous." Her voice cracked when she spoke. "I'm worried about him, he's worried about me. What a pair we are."

"You okay?" Ty touched the back of her

hand. Just a quick, gentle brush of his fingertips

Laying her head back, she stared at the sky. "I know it has nothing to do with you, but ever since you arrived, my life's been turned upside down."

He didn't ask about Lani and how much she'd contributed to Adele's topsy-turvy state. "I understand. It was like that for me last December when my horse was injured. I felt like I'd lost control of my life, and nothing I did seemed to help."

"What happened to your old horse?"

"I gave him to a buddy of mine for his teenage girls."

"So, he's not permanently crippled?"

"No. But he can't be used for anything except easy riding, which makes him a perfect family horse."

Ty held out his beer, offering her another sip. She declined with a shake of her head.

Too bad.

"What made you decide to turn Seven Cedars into a guest ranch?" he asked.

She relaxed, maybe for the first time that day. "I became serious about roping in college. Entering local jackpots was a way for me to make extra money, especially during the summers."

"You won a lot?"

"Yeah, I did." The hint of a smile touched her lips. "I would talk to the other competitors about where they were getting their training. A lot of them wished they had access to a more intensive program, one with equipment like professional ropers."

"And Cowboy College was born."

"Pop came up with the name." Her expression softened. "I was so nervous when I suggested the idea to him. I'd spent two months putting a business plan together, with the help of one of my instructors. But Pop, he was behind me one hundred percent from the beginning."

"Sounds like he's always been there for you."

"Always." She stood. "I think I'll go check on him. If he'll let me."

"I should get going." Ty also stood. "I've got an early class, and my teacher is a stickler for starting on time."

Her eyes warmed. "I really appreciate all you did for Pop."

"If you need anything, just call. I don't mind coming back."

"Thanks."

"Let me give you my cell number."

"I already have it."

He extended his hand. "Let me plug it into your phone. Save you a trip to the main lodge to look it up."

"I have it," she repeated in a quiet voice.

Pleasure shot through Ty as the implications of her statement sunk in.

"I'll be right back." She cut past him and went inside, but not before he caught sight of her pink-tinged cheeks.

He waited for her in the kitchen. She returned shortly, brandishing a key ring.

"I'll drive you back to your cabin."

They took Pop's old pickup. Ty wished the ride would last longer than it did. Too soon, their evening together ended.

"I hope I'm not one of those things that has turned your life upside down," he said, referring to her earlier remark.

Their gazes held.

"You are," she murmured.

He was surprised she admitted even that much. "I'm sorry. That wasn't my intention."

"Don't be." She shifted the truck from Neutral to Reverse. "I'm not entirely sure I didn't need a good shaking up."

He considered her remark long after she'd left, hoping it meant what he thought it did.

Chapter 7

Ty watched as a truck and horse trailer bearing the Maitland Ranch logo rolled past the open area in front of the barns. Maintaining a steady speed of five miles an hour, it continued to the pasture designated for visitor parking. The distance was too great for Ty to identify the driver of the truck, but his gut told him it was Garth Maitland, and that the two of them were in for a rematch today.

Friendship aside, this time Ty intended to win. Garth also wouldn't have it any other way.

On the second Saturday of every month, Cowboy College hosted a roping jackpot competition. Unlike professional rodeos, jackpots were open to anyone, regardless of gender. Participants paid an entry fee and competed against other individuals ranked the same as them. At the end of the competition, the pot was divided among the top three competitors in each group. The more participants, the bigger the pot—and the tougher the competition.

Ty couldn't wait to put into practice everything he'd learned since coming to Wyoming, and have his best time ever on Hamm.

"What are you standing there for?" Pop hobbled toward Ty. "That horse of yours won't saddle himself."

"You're right." Ty started off toward the barn, then slowed when he realized Pop was tagging along. "How you feeling?"

"The next person to ask me that is going to feel the sole of my boot in their arse when I kick them off this place."

"Better, then?"

"I slipped in the dang mud. Not like I fell off the roof."

The fall might have been minor, but not the aftereffects. Pop's arthritis had flared, confining him to the couch for several days. He'd finally gotten up and around yesterday, refusing to miss the monthly jackpot.

"Looks like we got a decent turnout," Ty commented.

"Right decent."

They entered the barn, the shade offering immediate relief from the midafternoon sun beating down. The spectators filling the bleachers were already cooling themselves with whatever they could convert into a makeshift fan, and guzzling cold drinks from the snack bar, run by the local Boy Scout troop.

"Garth Maitland's here," Pop said.

"I saw."

"He'll be riding his new horse. One he's never roped on before."

Ty opened Hamm's stall door. The big sorrel was raring to go and pawed the ground relentlessly while Ty snapped on the halter. "Garth's horse any good?"

"So I'm told."

Adrenaline built in Ty while he saddled Hamm. He ignored it, focusing all his mental energies on the upcoming jackpot. He'd learned long ago that the way to win was to treat every competition, big or small, local or National, like a World Championship.

"You're busy." Pop clapped Ty on the back. "How 'bout I catch up with you later."

Ty had momentarily forgotten he wasn't alone. "Any good advice before you go?" he asked, mounting Hamm.

Pop rolled the toothpick he was always chewing on from one side of his mouth to the other. "Forget about Garth. The only person you need to be concentrating on is yourself."

Ty nodded. He was right.

"You can beat him."

"Thanks for the vote of confidence."

Pop chuckled. "Well, a piece of humble pie wouldn't hurt Garth Maitland none."

Ty couldn't agree more.

At a slight pressure of his legs, Hamm trotted briskly from the barn. "See you at the winner's table," Ty called over his shoulder.

Outside, he made straight for the warm-up arena. From the nearby bleachers, the crowd cheered as the first group finished. Participants in the second group were lining up behind the boxes, while wranglers readied the calves.

Hamm, picking up on Ty's mood, shook his head and snorted, his front feet dancing.

"He's ready to go."

Ty looked up and smiled. He hadn't seen much of Adele since the night at Pop's house. "We both are." He pulled on the reins, slowing down so she could fall in step beside him.

"Where's Bella?" he asked, indicating the unfamiliar bay gelding she was riding.

"With her owner. He's giving her a go today."

"I'd like to see that."

"You will," she answered smoothly. "He's competing against you."

Realization dawned on Ty, and he smiled at his own gullibility. "You've been training her for Garth."

"Worried?"

"Not at all."

"You sound pretty sure of yourself."

Did he? The truth was his ego hadn't fully recovered from his loss to Garth last December. If he lost again today, he didn't want Adele knowing he'd failed despite having a newly acquired weapon in his arsenal.

"Care to make a wager?" he asked.

"Shouldn't you be talking to Garth?"

"I'm not interested in having dinner with him."

"Dinner!"

The idea had been a spontaneous one, but the more Ty thought about it, the more he liked it. "If I win, you take me to dinner."

"And if you lose?"

"I take you to dinner."

She pondered the wager. "That sounds more like a win-win situation for you."

It could be for both of them. "You want to raise the stakes?"

"Change them."

And here he thought she was going to turn him down. "To what?"

"You win, I go to dinner with you."

"Take me," he corrected.

"Okay, take you."

"And if I lose to Garth?"

Her eyes glinted with michief. "You teach the beginners' class for one week."

Ty's hand must have jerked on the reins, for Hamm suddenly slowed and bobbed his head. He didn't like being restrained.

"You kidding?"

"Not in the least." She smirked, obviously having fun with this.

"Why? Are you taking a vacation?"

"No. I just think the students would benefit, learning from a professional."

"The bet seems a little lopsided."

"Only if you're afraid of losing."

That got him, which was probably what she'd intended. "You're on. Make sure you have plenty available on your credit-card limit, because I have expensive tastes," he said, and broke into a slow trot.

Her laughter followed him as he circled the arena.

At the gate, Ty came face-to-face with Garth Maitland riding the paint mare. Both men nodded. Garth wore a wide, confident grin. Ty didn't let it faze him.

"Good luck, pal."

"Same to you."

This, Ty thought as he continued on, was going to be an interesting jackpot…for many reasons. And he had never been more ready.

Adele didn't stand on the fence railing behind the box with the other ropers. She'd be welcome; that wasn't the reason. Mostly, she didn't want Ty to see how nervous she was, waiting for him and Garth to finish their runs. To avoid any potential embarrassment to herself, she waited—make that hid—in the announcer's booth. While old Larry Fisher provided color commentary, his wife, along with the help of their oldest granddaughter, monitored the electronic timekeepers and kept the scores. If they were curious about Adele's presence in the booth, they didn't say.

Each contestant was allowed three turns.

Their scores were then added together and averaged. The person with the highest average was the winner. After two rounds, Garth led, with Ty coming in a close second. Chase, a newcomer, wasn't far behind in third place. It remained anybody's game.

She still wasn't sure she wanted Ty to win or lose. Beating Garth would do Ty good and restore some of his lost confidence. On the other hand, Adele had worked hard training Bella, and the horse was performing well. A win for Garth could potentially bring her new clients.

There was also the matter of her bet with Ty. Having dinner with him would be a mistake. Mind-boggling kissing and long, lingering glances aside, he was leaving soon. Regardless of how attracted she was to him, and she was seriously attracted, she wasn't about to engage in a temporary fling. Her mother had done enough of that for both of them.

Try as she might, however, Adele couldn't put the idea of dinner with Ty from her mind. Joe from Phoenix, as Pop had pointed out recently, was Adele's last serious romance. Sadly, it hadn't ended well. For either of them. Mainly because she wouldn't leave Seven Cedars.

Nothing had changed since then. She was as rooted at the ranch as always.

Anticipation at the final outcome of the jackpot had her standing on her toes to see better. Garth rode into the box and positioned Bella. Chase had taken his run moments before, and currently held the first place position. Dismounting, he hopped onto the arena fence alongside his buddies to wait out the rest of the competition.

Down in the arena, the gate to the chute flew open, releasing the calf. Garth followed in hot pursuit. Bella performed flawlessly. Even so, Adele tensed. Seconds later, it was all over. Prompted by his wife, Larry called out Garth's time, which was quickly added to his other two times to determine his final standing.

"That run, ladies and gentlemen," Larry said, his voice blaring from the speaker, "will put this here young man in first place."

Adele hadn't doubted the outcome. The question was, could Garth maintain it?

"Our last contestant for the day is Ty Boudeau." The crowd applauded. "Come on, folks," Larry coaxed, "don't be stingy. This cowboy needs more encouragement than that if he's going to take home the prize money." The audience broke into cheers.

Adele chewed on her bottom lip, studying Ty's every move as he lined up his horse in the box.

Why had she agreed to such a stupid bet?

Larry's wife swiveled around in her chair. "You doing okay, honey?" she asked Adele.

"Yeah, fine."

"You sure? 'Cause you've been fidgeting something awful."

Had she? Adele willed herself to relax.

Her efforts were wasted. A moment later, the calf sprang from the chute. Hamm went from zero to sixty in one second flat. Ty raised his arm high and threw his rope. It sailed through the air like an arrow, straight and true.

Her hands balled into tight fists, Adele watched Ty jump from Hamm's back and hit the ground at a dead run. In the next instant, he'd roped the calf and was throwing his arms up in the air even as he climbed to his feet.

She knew without looking that his time was a good one. Better than his first two runs. A glance at the digital display confirmed it, as did Larry's announcement.

"Ladies and gentlemen, weren't that a pretty run? Give it up for Mr. Ty Boudeau. Your winner today."

Happiness for Ty swelled inside Adele.

This competition might be nothing more than a two-bit local jackpot, but he'd needed the win. To prove he still had what it took. To prove he'd picked the right horse when he bought Hamm. To prove coming to Cowboy College was the right decision.

Larry turned away from the microphone. "Adele, tell Pop when he's got a second—"

"I'll get him for you."

She used the excuse to flee the announcer's booth. Only it wasn't Pop she went looking for when she reached the bottom of the stairs.

Ty wasn't hard to locate. A group of people, mostly fellow students and wranglers he'd come to be friends with, surrounded him and Hamm, offering their congratulations, shaking his hand and giving him hugs. Adele held back, a sudden and acute bout of shyness cementing her feet to the ground.

Slowly, the group thinned. Before the last person had departed, a lone cowboy approached. Garth Maitland. Adele was relieved to see he was wearing his usual grin.

"Good run, Boudeau." Garth extended his hand.

Ty shook it. "You, too."

"It'll be better at the Buffalo Bill Rodeo."

"I'm counting on it."

"Why don't you come by my place this week? Check out the facilities."

"I'd like that."

"Bring Adele with you."

Ty glanced over, caught her gaze and winked, giving her reason to think he'd known all along she was standing there. "I will."

Humph! What made him so convinced she'd go?

Because she wanted to, and he'd probably seen as much in her eyes.

"Give me a call," Garth told Ty, then turned in Adele's direction. Touching his fingers to his hat, he said, "See you later, Dellie."

Great. He'd known she was there all along, too.

Eventually, the last of Ty's fans left. The bleachers had emptied out and the Boy Scouts were packing up the snack bar. Only Ty and Adele remained. She stood there, still unsure what to do or say. He didn't seem to share her problem. Tugging on Hamm's reins, he closed the distance separating them, a happy smile stretching across his face.

"I'll start tomorrow, if you want."

"Start what?" she asked.

"Teaching the beginners' class."

"Why? You won."

"Yeah, but I'd like to, anyway. I've been working with Mike, giving him some pointers, and enjoying it."

"Really?"

"Took me by surprise, too."

"Seriously, Ty. You're not under any obligation. And you're here to work on your own skills."

He wasn't taking her to dinner. The stab of disappointment cutting through her was far stronger than she would have liked it to be.

"I owe you that much."

"For what?"

"Figuring out that Hamm takes aim with his right eye." Ty scratched behind his ear, the boyish gesture charming Adele. "The thing is, I was scared. Thinking somehow I'd lost it. Roping came so easy for me on my other horse. I took that for granted. The harder I tried with Hamm, the more I screwed up. Overcompensating, I suppose. Whatever was going wrong, I kept getting more and more tangled up in it. Coming here, focusing on the fundamentals, well, it's cleared my head and put me back on track."

Adele could see the admission hadn't come easy for Ty, and she valued it that much more.

"I'm glad." She returned his smile with a tentative one of her own.

In every direction, wranglers were hard at it, moving the calves to their regular pens, feeding the stock and cleaning up the arena. On the other side of the bleachers, Pop and Larry conversed. Too late, Adele remembered she hadn't informed her grandfather that the announcer wanted to speak to him.

"So, how's seven-thirty?" Ty asked, distracting her. "Does that give you enough time to change and get ready?"

"For what?"

"Dinner tonight."

"But I thought…you said you'd teach the beginners' class."

"That's a favor." He eased closer. And though he didn't touch her, Adele swore the bare skin on her forearms tingled as if stroked. "I still won."

Yes, he had.

"I intend to collect my dinner date," he added.

She could decline. Ty had coerced her into the bet, and she doubted he'd insist on holding her to it if she flatly refused.

"Seven-thirty will be fine," she answered

in a low voice. "I'll meet you in front of the main lodge."

Ty shook his head, his eyes glinting. "Nothing doing. This is a date. I'll pick you up at your place."

"All…right." She swallowed. "See you then."

"I'm looking forward to it."

So, Adele realized, was she. More than she should.

Chapter 8

Flowers.

Adele accepted the bouquet—fresh picked and tied with a ribbon—from Ty's outstretched hand, her movements tentative.

"Thank you."

As she cradled them to her chest, she tried to recall when a man had last given her flowers. The only incident to come to mind was a pink carnation corsage at her senior prom.

That long ago?

"Come in," she said, and stepped back to admit him, hoping he didn't notice the tiny catch in her voice.

He glanced around her smallish but, she liked to think, comfy living room. "Nice."

"Let me put these in water." The excuse was a good one and got her the minute she needed to compose herself.

Why didn't men give her flowers? Was it their unromantic nature? Her hesitancy to commit to a serious relationship? Maybe she was too much of a tomboy, and men assumed she didn't like flowers.

Except for Ty.

Her heart melted a little as she pulled a glass jar from the kitchen cupboard, filled it with water and arranged the flowers. Smiling to herself, she set them in the center of the table, then moved them to the breakfast bar, where she could see them first thing in the morning when she stumbled in from the bedroom.

"I'd have brought you roses, but there's no florist in Markton."

At the sound of Ty's voice behind her, she momentarily froze. "These are lovely," she said, covering her reaction.

The flowers were perfect, in fact.

Repositioning a daisy that wasn't out of place to begin with, she swallowed and turned to face him.

He looked good, doing justice to his jeans and Western dress shirt, which hugged his broad shoulders. The only place to eat a sit-down dinner in Markton was the Spotted Horse Saloon, and cowboy wear was practically required to get in the door. She'd picked her newest pair of jeans, her most flattering shirt, and left her usually bound hair loose to frame her face. Ty seemed to appreciate her changed appearance, given he'd yet to take his eyes off her.

"You ready?" She hesitated, feeling on unfamiliar territory. Entertaining men in her small apartment behind the main lodge wasn't something she did. "Or would you like a cold drink first?"

Cold drink! She mentally kicked herself for sounding like a waitress.

"We should probably get a move on." Ty flashed her a disarming smile. "We've got eight-o'clock reservations."

"Reservations?"

"It's Saturday night. I figured the place would be packed after the jackpot, and I wanted to make sure we got a table."

Ty was going out of his way to make their date special.

And it *was* a date, despite starting out as a bet. Her tingling insides confirmed it.

"Let me grab my purse."

Outside, Ty opened the passenger door of his truck for her and supported her elbow as she climbed in. Adele was about to protest that she climbed in and out of trucks all day long and didn't need help. At the last second, she shut her mouth and just enjoyed his chivalrous treatment.

Fifteen minutes later, they reached the Spotted Horse Saloon. Adele expected the place to be crowded, and she wasn't disappointed. It took them as long to find a parking spot and walk to the front entrance as to drive there.

"We have a reservation," Ty told the young hostess. "For Boudeau."

"Right this way, please."

Piped in country and western music accompanied them to a dark booth tucked in the corner. The band was scheduled to take the stage soon, and by nine o'clock the place would be hopping.

Ty stood and waited while Adele slid into the booth. He sat beside her—close—and the hostess passed them menus.

"Enjoy your meal."

Ty squinted at the menu, not easy to read in the dim light. "Are the specials any good?"

"Actually, most everything is." The cowboy-type fare at the Spotted Horse was simple but tasty. "I like the grilled chicken, and the fish and chips aren't bad."

Their dinner progressed comfortably, and the mood, much to Adele's relief, was definitely casual, with conversation centering mostly on Cowboy College and the students.

"We'll be taking a group of whoever wants to go to the Buffalo Bill Stampede Rodeo," she mentioned, while buttering a roll. "Pop, of course, wouldn't miss it."

"I'm already entered. Tie-down roping and team roping."

"Who's your partner for team roping?"

"A buddy of mine. Louis Garcia."

"I've heard of him. He's good."

She thought she might have detected a bit of tension in the lines around Ty's mouth. Was he nervous about competing? It was hard to tell over the mounting noise, a combination of the lively crowd and the band warming up on the stage. Adele recognized several ranch guests among the saloon patrons, as well as locals and out-of-town jackpot contestants. From where they sat, she could see almost as many people packed into the bar area.

"I don't think you ever told me what you do when you're not rodeoing." She fully expected him to answer horse trainer or wrangler or stock breeder. Those professions went hand in hand with rodeoing. She didn't see him following in his parents' footsteps by going into real estate.

"I apprentice at a saddle shop."

"Seriously?" She imagined a small, independently owned shop like the ones she'd visited before. "I don't remember ever reading that about you."

"You've read up on me?" A twinkle lit his eyes.

"I subscribe to horse and rodeo magazines. You're in them." She didn't mention the online searches she'd conducted before he'd arrived in Markton, afraid—make that *convinced*—it would go to his head.

"You're in them, too."

She felt his gaze on her and cleared her throat. "So, you build saddles?" she asked, as casually as if asking if he built bookcases in his spare time.

"A few. Mine, for one. Pop has a couple of old Charlie's."

"He does?" She stopped chewing. Pop owned a lot of custom-built saddles. But Ty had used only one, and she'd recognized the maker immediately. Could it be? "What's the name of the shop?"

"Kingston Saddlery."

"As in Charles Kingston?" She almost choked on her chicken. "You're kidding!"

Ty broke into an amused grin. "Not at all."

There wasn't a serious horse enthusiast alive who hadn't heard of Kingston Saddlery, and many wanted to own what was considered to be one of the finest custom built saddles available.

"That's where you work?"

"Yep. When I'm not rodeoing."

"And you make saddles. Actually *make* them?"

He laughed. "I actually make them. Though I'm still considered an apprentice. If you ask old Charlie, he's not sure I'll ever amount to anything else."

"How come you never said anything?"

"It's not a secret. Just something I don't publicize. Old Charlie's shop is one of the few places I can go and just be myself." His voice dropped. "So's Seven Cedars."

"Wow." Adele shook her head dumbly, still absorbing Ty's remarkable news.

"Is it so hard to believe I'm learning a

trade?" He turned his head and eyed her with a mixture of humor and curiosity.

"Well, saddle construction does take a lot of…" She scrunched her mouth to one side.

"Skill? Craftsmanship? Ingenuity?"

"I was going to say patience."

That earned her another laugh.

"And meticulous attention to detail. I suppose you also have to be good with your hands."

"You have no idea."

Too late, she realized her mistake. He immediately sobered, and the comfortable mood that had prevailed up till now vanished.

Oh, brother. She'd stepped right into that.

"Much as I like rodeoing, chances are I won't be doing it forever," Ty said philosophically around a bite of fish. "I may need a backup career."

Adele breathed easier at the change of subject.

"Besides, I'd like to be on road less, some day. Put down roots. Get married and have a couple of kids."

So much for breathing easier.

"I know a lot of guys—and women, too—who leave their families for months at a time, but I couldn't do it. Raising kids is hard enough for two people. It's got to be darn near impossible for one." He paused, suddenly catching himself. "I'm sorry, I wasn't criticizing. Your dad and mom—"

"It's okay. I agree with you." Adele tried to maintain a light tone. "I wouldn't want to be married to someone who was on the road for months at a time, either." And she wouldn't, not after seeing what that lifestyle had done to her parents' marriage. To her.

"When I do finally have kids," Ty continued, his gaze meeting hers, "I want to be there every moment. From the first visit to the baby doctor to the day they graduate and leave home."

Adele couldn't look away if she tried.

Fortunately, the band chose that moment to begin the first set. Despite being good, the music was loud, and limited conversation. Ty made up for it by sending her smoldering glances between bites. Adele polished off the last of her meal in a rush. This thing happening between them, whatever it was, couldn't go anywhere, and she needed to put a halt to it once and for all.

She was just setting her fork down and hoping they'd be leaving soon when the band launched into a slow number, one of George Strait's more popular hits.

"Let's dance," Ty abruptly said.

"I…ah…"

Her senior prom was the last time a man had given her flowers. It was also the last time she'd danced to such a slow song.

He stood and tilted his head toward the band. "Come on. I won't bite. Not on a first date, anyway."

Was he joking?

Walking ahead of him, Adele tried to convince herself she wasn't making a huge mistake. Just look what had happened the last time Ty had held her in his arms.

"Relax," he said into her ear, and pressed his palm against the center of her back.

She tried. It wasn't easy. The man smelled too darn sexy for his own good.

"Afraid I'm a little more comfortable on a horse than the dance floor," she confessed.

"It's not all that different than riding. You just have to find the rhythm and settle in."

He couldn't be more wrong. Dancing was entirely different than riding.

On horseback, she was in complete control. Wrapped in Ty's arms, she was a stick being carried along by a rushing, storm-swollen river.

But after an awkward minute, she did indeed find the rhythm, and stopped inhaling sharply every time their bodies gently collided, either from a misstep on her part or another couple bumping into them. No sooner did the tension start to ebb than the song ended.

"Wait," Ty told her when she began to pull away.

"The song's over," she murmured. The realization that she rather enjoyed staying right where she was made her nervous all over again.

"They'll play another one."

And the band did, this one also slow. Had Ty known?

Without any prompting on his part, she slipped back into his embrace, her earlier suspicions that they were headed for trouble solidifying into absolute certainty. He felt good. Strong and sure of himself. And those hands he'd bragged about were holding her as if he had no intention of ever letting her go.

As the song played on, she discovered that following his steps wasn't all that hard. When he lowered his head to brush his temple against hers, she didn't retreat or tell him to stop. Stranger still, when his hand moved from the center to the small of her back, she turned her head and rested her cheek on his chest as if she'd done it a thousand times before.

Maybe her lack of finesse on the dance floor had less to do with talent and more to do with not having the right partner.

As they moved to the seductive beat, Ty's heart rate slowly increased. She could sense the pounding more than she could hear it over the loud music. When her fingers walked gingerly from his shoulder to the back of his neck, his heart rate accelerated even more.

People were looking at them, Adele noticed through slitted eyes and a dreamy haze that had begun to surround her. Not that she could blame them. As Pop had pointed out recently, she hardly dated, much less glided across a crowded dance floor in the arms of an incredibly attractive rodeo star. One who also worked for the best custom saddle and leather shop in the Southwest.

She was still trying to wrap her brain around that piece of news when Ty suddenly swung her in a half circle in order to avoid colliding with Mike and Sandy.

"Whew!" It took Adele a moment to regain her balance.

"Sorry," Mike called over the music before he and his wife were swallowed by the other dancers.

"You okay?" Ty asked.

Adele looked up at him, and her own heart began racing. At close range and in the dim light of the honky-tonk, his brown eyes were dark as ebony. They studied her with the intensity of a man with an agenda. An agenda that involved the two of them alone in a secluded place, those talented hands of his discovering the curve of her hips and the texture of her skin.

Adele averted her gaze. She had little experience with the kind of supercharged sexual currents running between her and Ty.

He let go of her hand and, tucking a finger beneath her chin, lifted her face to his. Dancing became impossible, so they stopped, staring into each other's eyes right there in the middle of the dance floor. The people moving beside them were just blurs to Adele, who only had eyes for Ty.

Leaning down until their foreheads touched, he said, "I want to take you home. Right now."

She withdrew slightly, his remark swiftly bringing her back to her senses.

"I—I don't… I can't…"

He wanted her. And she returned the feelings. But she wasn't ready for *that*. Not yet.

He looked stricken. "I wouldn't take advantage of you, Adele." He blew out a breath and, giving her a gentle tug, pulled her back into his arms. "God, I screwed that up." They started dancing again. "I want to kiss you." He caught her gaze once more. "You can't imagine how much." His mouth curved up in an apologetic smile. "I just didn't want to do it here, and figured if I took you home, I'd have my chance."

"I see," she muttered softly.

"This keeps getting worse and worse. I should just shut up."

"No. It's all right." Adele gathered her courage and made a leap she never had before with a man. "Because I want you to kiss me."

"You do?" Ty's grin widened.

She nodded, and said, "Let's get out of here," just as the music stopped.

Unfortunately, several people were close enough to hear her. Including Mike and Sandy, who both smiled knowingly.

"Good idea." Mike waggled his eyebrows

and flashed Sandy a look that left no question as to his own intentions.

Adele groaned inwardly. She rigorously strived to keep her private life just that. Tonight, however, she'd broken that rule.

"You've got an early morning tomorrow," Ty said loudly enough for everyone to hear. "And Pop's waiting for you." With a gentlemanly touch to her back, he guided her off the dance floor.

"Thank you," she said, when they reached their booth. Ty had done his best to make it clear he and Adele weren't spending the night together. She liked him for that. More than liked him.

"I'd say I was sorry, except I'm not going to get in the habit of apologizing, or thinking I should apologize, every time I kiss you."

Something about his tone caused a tingle to skip lightly up her spine. Almost like the gliding of fingertips. *His* fingertips.

"You say that as if we're going to kiss a lot."

"A man can hope."

The dinner tab had been placed on their table while they were dancing. Adele reached for it, but Ty beat her to the punch.

"Hey, I'm supposed to pay."

"I'll get it."

"We had a bet."

"You can pay next time."

"Who says there's going to be a next time?"

"There is if you owe me dinner."

"You're impossible!"

Ty removed his wallet and place several bills inside the folder containing the dinner tab. His gaze held hers as he replaced it on the table. "Don't think this gets you out of kissing me tonight."

"It never crossed my mind," she said softly, reeling from more of those sexual currents.

Despite her earlier vow to keep her personal life private, she didn't object when Ty clasped her hand in his. Together, they wove through the throng of boisterous patrons.

With each step, she tried convincing herself not to get involved with Ty. His return to the rodeo circuit loomed ahead. Unless she could be satisfied with seeing him a few days here and a few days there, engaging in a romantic relationship could only end with her being hurt.

No amount of warning, however, lessened the anticipation building inside her at the prospect of their next kiss. How could she refuse him? Especially when she might not have another chance?

To reach the front entrance, they had to pass the bar area. Typical for a Saturday night, people stood two and three deep. If a big burly man hadn't chosen that exact moment to back away from the bar, Adele might have left without ever having spotted her mother parked on a stool near the end.

The sight of Lani hefting a beer wasn't enough to stop Adele in her tracks. She'd seen her mother in bars before. It was the man she sat next to, with her head bent close to his in what was clearly an intimate conversation, that left Adele chilled.

Henry Parkman, owner of the feed store. *Married* Henry Parkman. And until this moment, Adele had thought him happily married.

His wedded state, however, didn't seem to make a difference to Lani. She flashed her white teeth at him before tipping her head back and laughing uproariously.

Adele's mother had always gone after men; that was nothing new. Somewhere along the line she'd apparently moved to married men. Adele felt sick to her stomach.

Every thought fled her head save one: getting the hell out of the Spotted Horse. Legs shaking, she sidestepped Ty and brushed past another couple in her haste to reach the entrance, her escape fueled by an incessant roaring in her ears.

"You don't have to get out," Adele said when Ty opened his truck door and pocketed his keys.

"I'd like to walk you to your door, if you don't mind."

He assumed the good-night kiss they'd teased about at the Spotted Horse—the one that had sent his pulse skyrocketing—wouldn't materialize. That didn't stop him from wanting to see her safely inside.

Adele's mood had plummeted the moment she saw her mother with Henry Parkman, the owner of the feed store. And understandably so. Ty had remained silent on the subject during the short ride home, commenting on the weather and upcoming rodeo, and not pressuring her when she didn't respond. It had been obvious from the day he first saw Lani in the barn with Pop that any discussion of Adele's mother was off-limits.

From somewhere nearby, one of the ranch's

many dogs barked. Ty sat behind the steering wheel, absently tapping a foot.

When Adele didn't immediately exit the truck, he waited another moment, then shut his door. She continued sitting in the passenger seat, staring into the darkness at a row of sprawling cottonwood trees, standing like a black wall against a silver sky.

Strange behavior for someone who'd been in an all-fired hurry to get home not twenty minutes earlier.

Okay, maybe she did want to talk. Or not be alone. When she still didn't move or speak, he hunkered down in his seat, pushed back his cowboy hat and scratched his forehead. The intricate workings of a woman's mind had often eluded Ty, and he'd long ago developed a system to use in situations like this one. When in doubt, wait and say nothing.

"I'm sorry," Adele finally muttered.

"For what?"

"I know this isn't how you expected the evening to end."

"Don't sweat it."

"From the day my mom arrived, I've been trying to figure out why she showed up. I should have guessed it was to find a new man. She doesn't go long without one. I just hadn't realized she'd lowered her already low standards and was including married men in her pickings." Hurt and disappointment roughened Adele's voice.

Ty decided to go out on a limb. "Don't take this wrong, but are you sure your mother was going after Henry Parkman?"

Adele turned her head to gawk at Ty with disbelief. "You saw the two of them at the bar."

"I did." He scratched his forehead again. "Can't say there was much going on between them other than talking and laughing."

"If she'd been sitting any closer to him, she'd have been in his lap."

"The place was pretty crowded. Hard not to sit close to someone with people crammed in all around you."

"Why are you defending her?"

"I'm not defending her. Only saying I didn't see anything more than two people having a friendly conversation."

"Yeah. *Real* friendly. That's how it always starts with her."

Ty let the remark pass, returning to his original plan to say nothing. Women were talkers, he reminded himself, and men were fixers. She probably didn't want his advice, just a sounding board on which to vent her frustrations. At least, that was what his sisters used to tell him when he opened his mouth once too often with unsolicited advice.

Several more moments passed with Adele sitting silently. Ty leaned back, content to be patient, and determined to be what she needed, even if he couldn't figure out exactly what that was.

"You have a perfect family," she murmured, staring out the window again.

"I wouldn't call them perfect."

"Your mom and dad are still married after, what, thirty years?"

"Something like that."

"They not only raised three kids, they both have successful careers. I'd call that pretty perfect."

"They've had their share of rough patches." Some of them a direct result of Ty and a few rather rebellious teen years.

"My parents divorced when I was three." She heaved a sigh. "I don't really know why. My dad refused to talk about it, and the reasons my mom gave always sounded a bit…manufactured." Adele turned toward Ty. "Do people really grow apart?" Without waiting for him to answer, she resumed gazing out the window. "I think she just got tired of him." Adele's voice hitched. "Like she got tired of me."

"That's not true."

"How would you know?"

"All right, I don't." That's what he got for trying to say the right thing. Back to plan one: be quiet and listen.

"She left me here every chance she got. Every time she found a new man to latch on to. What kind of mom does that to her own kid?"

"Maybe she was trying to protect you."

"From what?" Adele asked, her expression incredulous.

Ty ground his teeth, cursing his inability to shut up.

"From *what?*" she repeated when he didn't respond.

He was probably going to regret it later, but answered her anyway. "From the lifestyle she was living. From the men she was with. From the constant liquor and partying and living on the road in a motor home or in a hotel room. I can't imagine any mother wanting to expose her child to that."

"Then why didn't she just stay home and get a regular job? Why did she dump me off at my father's or grandparents' every chance she got?"

"You should be asking your mother these questions."

Clearly, he'd blundered, for Adele sprang into action, wrenching open her door and jumping out.

Ty went after her, but she'd gotten a solid head start on him. He caught a break when she fumbled with her keys at the front door.

"Adele, I'm sorry." He came up beside her. "I shouldn't have said that." Dang it all, she was crying. "Oh, sweetheart." He placed a comforting hand on her shoulder.

She went into his arms so fast he momentarily lost his footing.

"I hate being one of those pathetic people with mommy issues," she said, her face buried in the front of his shirt.

"There's a reason Lani came here." Ty put an arm securely around Adele. When she didn't retreat, he tugged her closer.

"That's what Pop says, too," she muttered. "He thinks I should give her a chance to explain."

"Your grandfather's a smart man."

"Not about everything. He overdoes it and falls."

"Well, that's true."

Ty forced himself to concentrate. It was

hard holding Adele—feeling her body fitted snugly against his—and not responding. He ached to taste her lips, glide his palms along her supple curves. When his hand inadvertently slipped off her shoulder and down her back, he quickly pulled it away.

"You're right about me talking to my mom," Adele said, her head nestled in the crook of Ty's neck as if it belonged there. "It's just that we've never been close, and talking about anything serious…" She gave a small laugh. "We don't."

"When's the last time you tried?"

"I don't even remember. How sad is that?"

She sounded so forlorn, he couldn't resist, and placed a tender kiss on the top of her head.

Big mistake.

"Ty." She immediately pushed away from him.

"My fault, I got carried away."

"It's not that. I do…want to kiss you again." She settled her palms on his chest. "Just not when I'm all weak and weepy and an emotional mess. Been there, done that, and once was enough."

He brushed aside a stray lock of her hair. "I'm willing to wait."

Using the key still clutched in her hand, she

opened her front door. "Thanks for dinner. I really did have a nice time."

"Nice enough to do it again?"

"You're leaving soon."

"Which doesn't give us time to waste."

In response, she stood on tiptoe and kissed his cheek. He expected her to immediately retreat, but again she lingered, her lips soft on his skin. If she'd wanted to torture him, she couldn't have devised a more effective method.

"Good night, Ty," she whispered.

Unable to control himself, he dipped his head and inhaled the incredible scent of her. Sweet and flowery, like peach blossoms.

"Good night, Adele."

Difficult as it was, he stepped back. Giving her one last look, he touched his fingers to the brim of his hat and returned to his truck.

On the drive to his cabin, he remembered she hadn't given him an answer about going on another date. He wasn't worried. She'd mentioned wanting to kiss him again.

And Ty had every intention of taking her at her word.

Chapter 9

Adele sat at the folding picnic table outside the camper she and Pop were sharing during their long weekend at the Buffalo Bill Cody Rodeo. Cheers from the crowd carried across the parking lot to the open field where they and a hundred or so other people had constructed a makeshift RV park. Though it was normally reserved for contestants, Pop and Adele stayed there because of his long-standing involvement in rodeos and his previous championships.

Once a member of the rodeo community, always a member.

Pop opened the door of the camper and

climbed down the steps. While Adele had been woolgathering and listening to the distant cheers, he'd been inside taking a short, midafternoon nap.

"Aren't you going to mosey over and watch Ty compete?"

"I will soon." She knew from the schedule on the table that Ty's event wasn't starting for another twenty-five minutes.

"Have you seen him today?"

"Earlier. After the team roping."

As Pop sat down across from her, the lightweight picnic table seesawed, ceasing to move only when he did. "I bet he's mad at himself. A new partner and a new horse are a difficult combination."

Ty had partnered with an old friend for the event. They'd done passably well on Saturday, but bombed the final round today, making several avoidable mistakes.

"Don't tell that to Ty."

Pop chuckled. "I bet he's a nervous wreck about now."

"And doing a poor job of hiding it, from what Mike and Sandy tell me." Some of the students attending the rodeo had reported back to her, too.

"He'd better get ahold of himself if he wants to do well in tie-down roping."

"He will. He's a pro, and committed."

"I figured you'd be down there offering him moral support."

Adele ignored her grandfather's penetrating gaze. This was hardly the first hint he'd dropped that she and Ty had a romantic thing going.

They didn't. In fact, they'd spoken only in passing the last two weeks. He'd been busy teaching the beginners' class, practicing for the rodeo at every opportunity, and fussing over Hamm as if the horse were a newborn baby. She'd given Ty his space so as not to distract him.

Or so she told herself.

In truth, he'd asked some hard questions the night of their date—she'd stopped thinking of it as anything else—and seeing him only reminded her that she had no answers for the questions, and probably never would. Not without talking to her mother, as Ty and Pop had both suggested.

Except Adele could hardly bring herself to say hi to her mom, not after seeing her with Henry Parkman, and avoided her at all costs.

"Pop, why did my parents get divorced?"

His brows shot up. "Where in blue blazes did that come from?"

"I've been wondering about it ever since Mom showed up."

Lani hadn't accompanied the small group of students to the rodeo. Initially, Adele had been relieved; her mother wouldn't be attempting to attach herself to a new man. Then Adele panicked. What if Lani was staying home in order to be with Henry Parkman?

Adele rubbed her eyes and sighed. Ty was wrong. That conversation in the bar hadn't been casual. Adele had seen her mother in action too often not to know when she had her game on.

"What did your folks tell you?" Pop asked.

"Dad never talked about it."

"That doesn't surprise me. Warren was always one to keep his hurt to himself."

"Why did Mom leave him? Was he such a bad husband?" Adele had always suspected it was the other way around—that her mother was a bad wife.

"She did move out, but you couldn't fault her. Not really." Pop massaged the knuckles of one hand, then the other, a sign his arthritis was acting up. "They were young when they got married. And Warren was on the road a lot. I don't think rodeo life is good for a marriage."

Adele couldn't agree more. It was yet another strike against Ty, despite her attraction to him.

"Add a baby, plus a drinking problem on top of that, and it's a lot for two inexperienced kids to handle."

Adele frowned. "Mom's always liked to party, I know, but I don't remember her drinking *that* much. Not while I was around."

"She didn't. Warren's the one with the drinking problem."

"What?" Adele almost slipped from her seat. "Dad doesn't drink. Not a drop."

"He used to. Like a fish. That's what put an end to his rodeo career. One too many drinks, way too many losses. A shame, too, because he had real talent."

"I… I can't believe it."

Sorrow shone in Pop's eyes. "Warren went on a binge to beat all binges about a year after he and your mom separated. Crashed his truck into a billboard pillar and damn near killed himself."

"Where?"

"On the highway twenty miles outside of Markton."

"I don't remember any accident."

"Your mom took you to Cheyenne, where she had some friends. After the accident, she brought you to the ranch, but didn't tell you about your dad being all banged up. You were just a tyke, and she thought seeing your father in such bad shape would give you nightmares. He recovered and has been on the straight and narrow ever since."

Adele sat back, her head swimming. All these years, she'd assumed her father left Wyoming and ran off to Texas to escape her mother. Or, as a small part of her heart had feared, because he hadn't wanted her. In reality, he'd done so in order to turn his life around.

"Why didn't he tell me?"

"It's hard for some folks to admit their mistakes. Especially to their kids. It's one of the reasons he didn't fight your mother for joint custody of you, much as I wanted him to. He found a good woman who keeps him in line. Reminders of his past, well, they seem to tempt him too much. He falls into old habits."

"I'm not a child anymore," Adele said with a trace of bitterness. "Yet he still refuses to include me in his life."

"That goes both ways."

Pierced by guilt, she averted her glance.

"Someone's got to take the first step," Pop urged.

Hadn't Ty said almost the same thing about her mother?

Adele rubbed her temples, which were throbbing now from her taking in so much at once. Had she been wrong all these years about *both* her parents? The possibility sobered her.

"None of us likes the idea of being a disappointment to our children." Pop's expression softened. "Take it from me."

"You've never disappointed Dad. Or me."

"I did. When I let the ranch practically go to ruin after your grandmother passed."

"That was understandable."

"So is what happened to your parents."

Adele said nothing.

"Could be why your mother came back. Hoping to set things right with you."

She stared at the rodeo grounds across the parking lot. People and vehicles poured in and out, as they had all weekend long. Even at a distance, the tourists were easy to spot, with their shorts, T-shirts, sneakers and souvenirs. Children walked beside their parents, balloons bobbing at the end of strings.

"It took a lot of courage for Lani to show up," Pop said gently. "She had to know you'd still be mad at her."

"I thought you didn't like my mother."

"That's not true. I despised what she did to you, carting you off to some new place on a whim, leaving you on your father's doorstep or mine whenever the mood struck. But then, I knew she was unhappy and that Warren had caused a lot of it. I also remember her the way she was when your dad and she first met. Your mother was the prettiest, sweetest little gal."

No one, as far as Adele knew, had ever described her mother as pretty or sweet. She must have been, however. Pop didn't usually hand out compliments where Lani was concerned.

"Why are you telling me all this now? Why not before?"

"I wasn't altogether sure you'd listen."

Adele *was* listening. Understanding, however, was a different matter. "We're a miserable lot, when you think about it."

"Doesn't have to be that way. Which is why I let Lani stay." Pop reached across the table and patted Adele's hand. "It's not too late for you and your mother to mend some of those bridges."

"I don't know," Adele said wistfully. "I don't think I can, not while she's up to her old tricks."

"What tricks?"

"I saw her at the Spotted Horse last week with Henry Parkman."

The toothpick Pop had been rolling from side to side in his mouth stilled. "Are you sure?"

"Of course I'm sure."

"They were together?"

"Sitting at the bar, big as life."

"I can't believe that. Henry and Carmella have been together over twenty years."

"I know."

"He's devoted to her."

"When Mom goes after a man, she's hard to resist." Adele could still see Lani smiling up into Henry's face, hear her boisterous laughter. "I'm worried that's why she didn't come to the rodeo, so she could be with Henry without the rest of us around."

"Except he's here."

"He is?" Adele's eyes went wide.

"Him and Carmella both. The feed store's one of the sponsors."

"I haven't seen them all weekend." Though she had noticed the store's colorful banner hanging in the main arena.

"Well, they're here. You've probably been too busy with the students and Ty."

Adele wanted to object. She'd been so certain her mother had returned to her old ways.

"What did you see Henry and Lani doing at the Spotted Horse?" Pop asked.

"Sitting close. Talking. Laughing and smiling at each other."

"That all?"

"Don't say it like it's nothing." Adele scowled. "Mom was flirting with him, and he didn't seem to mind."

"Flirting is a far cry from having an affair."

"It's still wrong."

"Are you sure it wasn't the other way around? Henry could've been flirting with your mother."

Adele started to answer, then clamped her mouth shut.

Two people had now told her she may have been jumping to a wrong conclusion. As much as she hated to admit it, the possibility was looking more and more likely. Were her feelings for Lani so negative and slanted that she was quick to assume the worst?

Doubts came rushing in. Adele had been comfortable for years living with her anger at both her parents. Just because the time for change might be at hand didn't mean she was eager to embrace it.

A cheer went up in the stands. It was followed by the announcer's voice, telling the audience to stay seated for the final round of tie-down roping, due to start after a ten-minute break.

"We'd better get a move on." Pop rose from his seat, causing the small picnic table to see-saw again.

Adele also stood. Her grandfather could move only so fast, and they had a fair distance to cover—which gave her plenty of opportunity to think...and reconsider.

During the walk to the main arena, Adele pulled herself together, only half listening to Pop's chatter and half noticing the endless stream of people, participants and horses. Tantalizing aromas from the concession stands and brightly painted signs atop vendor booths vied for their attention. She practiced smiling, wanting to present a relaxed demeanor to the students sitting in the section of bleacher seats they'd reserved. Pop would head on down to the chutes and boxes to watch the tie-down roping and give last-minute advice to the participants he'd mentored through the years.

The first competitor had just finished his run by the time Adele climbed the bleacher stairs, saying hi to the students and hoping they didn't notice her distracted state. Luckily, their gazes were centered elsewhere.

She sat in the only available seat, which happened to be next to Mike and Sandy. They were leaving Cowboy College the next day, and Adele would be sad to see them go. They'd been two of the ranch's more enjoyable and memorable guests.

"I was pleased to hear about Pop," Mike said, leaning forward to converse with Adele around his wife.

"What about him?" She automatically searched for Ty, finally spotting him behind the chutes and boxes. He sat astride Hamm, waiting his turn and watching the competition from that vantage point.

"The report from his orthopedic surgeon."

Adele squinted curiously at Mike. "What report?"

"When he saw his doctor last week." Understanding and then embarrassment flashed across his face. "You don't know."

"What did the doctor say?"

Mike shook his head. "I'm sorry. I can't tell you."

"But he's not your patient."

"Even so." He looked miserable because of his blunder. "I thought Pop had discussed the report with you."

"Well, he didn't." At the moment, she wasn't sure who to be more agitated with, Pop or Mike.

"Ask him," Mike urged.

"Tell me this much. Do I have anything to be worried about?" Anything *more*. Between Ty's event and the revelations about her parents, she'd reached her stress limit for the day.

Mike broke into a grin, and repeated, "Ask him. But in the meantime, feel free to sleep easy tonight."

That much was a relief.

"Next up," the announcer called, his voice blaring from the speakers, "is a young man all the way from Missouri."

Young was right. He didn't look any older than nineteen. At twenty-seven, Ty was one of the older competitors. He was also one of the more experienced, and that counted in his favor.

When Adele glanced back over at the box, she noticed he was gone. She didn't think much about it, assuming he was warming up Hamm. But when Ty didn't reappear a few minutes later, she started to worry. His turn was fast approaching.

Great, yet another thing to weigh on her mind. She'd be glad when this weekend was over and she could go home, retreat to a quiet place and think things through. Maybe talk to her mother.

Maybe.

The sudden ringing of her cell phone took her by surprise. She tried but couldn't read the display in the bright sunlight. Giving up, she answered the call.

"Hello."

"Come meet me by the stock pens."

She recognized Ty's voice immediately, and a jolt shot through her. "What's wrong?"

"Just come. I need a favor." He sounded anxious.

Various scenarios played in her head. A problem with Hamm or an equipment mal-function. A last minute strategy powwow.

Something significant, or else why would Ty call her so close to his run?

"Be right there," she told him, already on her feet and squeezing past people on her way to the aisle.

Ty stood exactly where he said he'd be waiting, holding Hamm's reins. From a distance, everything looked fine. His equipment was intact, the horse appeared calm and uninjured, and Ty's features were composed, reflecting determination and—this was a good sign—confidence.

Adele wove in and out of the throng of people, hurrying to get to him as fast as she could. She didn't question her sense of urgency or why her heart was suddenly turning somersaults. The last forty-five minutes had delivered one emotional bombshell after another. The entire week, really. No wonder her nerves were a tangled mess and her anxiety level through the roof.

Anxiety? Or excitement?

No denying it. The small thrill winding through her as she drew close to Ty had more to do with attraction than trepidation. Much more.

At last she broke free from the crowd. Feeling like a fish escaping through a hole in a fisherman's net, she slowed down, covering the remaining thirty feet separating her and Ty at a walk. Until that moment, he'd been staring at the arena, his head cocked slightly to one side as he listened to the announcer's evaluation of the last contestant's run—a good one, according to the score. Ty would have to give everything he had and then some if he intended to win.

He must have sensed her approach, for he suddenly turned. When their gazes connected, his eyes lit up, then turned dark and smoldering. The small thrill became a rushing river of awareness. All at once, Adele knew why Ty had called her to meet him, and what he wanted. She didn't hesitate going to him.

Dropping the reins, he came forward. Luckily, Hamm was placid by nature outside the arena, because another horse might have spooked when Adele flung herself into Ty's open arms.

"I've been waiting two weeks for this," he said as his mouth came down on hers.

Only two weeks? It felt to Adele as if she'd been waiting forever. For this kiss. This moment. This man.

Forgetting all the obstacles facing them and

the fact that he was leaving soon, *very* soon, forgetting the crowd, which had dissolved into a soundless blur, she returned Ty's kiss with a passion matching his. Instinct told her he needed this connection to her, physical and emotional, in order to compete. Every bit as much as he needed the lariat tied to his saddle.

The sense of contentment stealing over her told her she needed it, too. Perhaps even more than he did, for all at once her world stopped rocking wildly and righted itself.

Offering no resistance to his bold advances, she molded her body to his, relishing the sensation of his hands firmly pressed into her back, his hard muscled length as he anchored her to him, and his tongue as it swept into her mouth.

She could only imagine the number of open stares they were garnering, but she didn't care. Every harsh breath he drew, every groan issuing from deep in his chest told her neither did he.

A loud, bawdy whoop penetrated her foggy brain, returning her to reality.

"Hey, Boudeau! Hate to break up the party but you're up soon. Better get a move on."

Ty broke off their kiss, his reluctance showing in his eyes. "I want to see you tonight."

"Another date?" she asked, still holding on to him.

"Okay."

The way he said "okay" gave her reason to think he'd had something else in mind.

So did she.

"All right."

He grinned.

"On one condition."

"What's that?" He bent as if to nuzzle her neck. Her next words stopped him.

"You take first in tie-down roping."

He lifted his head. "You think I can't?"

"Not at all. But if you want to see me tonight, you'd better be bringing that belt buckle with you."

"Be ready at seven." Letting go of her, he gathered the reins and mounted Hamm in one fluid motion. "And wear something sexy."

With that, he trotted off to the area behind the box.

Ignoring the snickering and gawking, Adele ran back to the bleachers and her seat.

She couldn't help feeling that Ty winning this event was more important than him getting back on track, and more significant than going on another date with him.

It seemed to Adele as if her whole life was suddenly poised to change.

Chapter 10

"Boudeau, you're up next!"

Ty nudged Hamm into place behind the box. The horse responded with the tiniest of cues, already in the zone and ready to go. Ty wished he could say the same for himself. Kissing Adele had affected his concentration—among other things.

That hadn't been his plan. Not intentionally. He'd only wanted to talk to her. Why, he wasn't sure now. Only that two weeks without close interaction had been too long. The need to see her, even briefly, before he went into the arena had been so powerful, he hadn't thought his actions through, simply punched in her number.

And she'd come. Just like that. Without requiring an explanation.

When he'd seen her hurrying toward him, eager anticipation brightening her expression, the part of his brain not a slave to logic had taken over, and he'd kissed her. *Really* kissed her. And it had wiped away every memory of every other woman before her.

He couldn't wait for tonight.

Except if he didn't get it together, and fast, there would be no "tonight" with her.

He had to take first place.

For her, but also for himself. Somewhere along the way, winning at roping and winning over Adele had become intermingled, and he didn't think he could separate the two.

"On deck, Boudeau."

"Sorry," Ty said, realizing his name had been called a second time. He urged Hamm closer to the box.

"You got this in the bag, son."

Ty glanced down to see Pop hobbling over. "That's what I'm hoping."

The older man gave Ty's leg an encouraging pat. "Billy Carpenter broke the barrier."

"Is that so?" Ty had missed Billy's run and

the penalty. It must have happened while he and Adele were kissing.

"The only ones left who can possibly beat you are Mitch Benson and Garth Maitland."

"I'm not worried about Benson," Ty said. Lifting his head to see over the crowd, he watched the man in question throw his rope. "He chokes under pressure."

Benson's toss sailed straight and true, but when he went to tie the calf's legs, his hand accidentally slipped, costing him precious seconds. The announcer commiserated and encouraged the audience to give him a round of applause.

"That leaves Garth," Ty said, his jaw tightening.

"He goes last."

"I know."

Taking no chances, Ty checked his equipment with the thoroughness of a heart surgeon preparing for a transplant operation.

"Boudeau!"

He only had to loosen his grip on the reins slightly, and Hamm charged forward into the box, ready to go. As the big animal settled in, Ty knew he'd been right to purchase him. There wasn't a better horse around or a better horse for him. They could win today.

Hell, they could go all the way to the National Finals Rodeo in December, where participants from all over the world competed.

Pop had followed Ty as far as the fence. One of the cowboys moved aside and made room for the older man, who hoisted himself onto the bottom rail with a grunt.

Ty barely noticed. He was too preoccupied rewinding his lariat into a coil for the third time and hefting it in his hand. He didn't stop until the lariat felt exactly right.

"This probably isn't the time to tell you," Pop said, loudly enough for Ty and everyone else to hear, "but I approve of you courting my granddaughter. If that's your intention."

Caught off guard, Ty looked up. Had Pop seen them kissing? "It is my intention, sir. But I have to bring home a buckle first."

Pop laughed till he choked. "She tell you that?"

"She did. And I think she's serious."

"Then you'd better have the run of your life."

Ty couldn't agree more.

He could feel the eyes of every man standing on or straddling the fence. They knew his history, many of them having seen him lose to Garth last year. They realized today could be, make that *was*, Ty's comeback. He wasn't going to disappoint them.

Or Adele.

"Good luck, Boudeau."

"You got it in the bag, Ty."

He settled deeper into his saddle, ignoring his buddies. They weren't expecting him to reply, anyway, understanding that he was getting himself where he needed to be mentally.

A last tug on his gloves. One more inspection of his lariat and the knot that secured it to his saddle horn. A final stretch of the pigging string before he placed it between his teeth. One more hat adjustment. With each action, he narrowed his concentration until all he saw, all that mattered was his horse, the calf and the wrangler manning the gate to the chute.

"Get ready, boy," he said under his breath, giving Hamm's neck a quick pat.

Long days of honing his skills, learning about himself and his horse, were about to pay off. A burst of confidence exploded inside him, growing stronger as if he'd drunk a magical elixir.

"Go." The single clipped word accompanied a brusque nod of his head.

The gate to the chute opened with a harsh

metallic swish. An instant after the calf escaped, Ty and Hamm were in motion, operating on pure adrenaline and instinct. Ty's arm came up in the air at just the right moment. The rope flew from his hand with precision and accuracy, sailing toward the running calf on a perfect gust of air. Even before the lasso reached its target, Ty was swinging his leg over the saddle, leaping off and hitting the ground at a dead run.

Hamm did his job, stepping backward and pulling the rope taut. Ty also did his job, sliding his hand along the rope as he ran forward. The instant the calf was down on its side, he wound the pigging string around its legs and threw his hands in the air to signal he was done.

He didn't need to hear the announcer or glance at the scoreboard to know he'd performed well. He could feel it in the thundering of his heart and the surge of energy racing through him.

Untying the calf, he collected his rope and pigging string, walked over to Hamm and gave the horse's neck another pat. "Thanks, partner."

Hamm bobbed his head up and down, then knocked his nose into Ty's shoulder. It seemed he was also happy with their run. The two of them made for the gate, Ty leading Hamm by the reins.

Applause broke out as Ty's official score appeared on the board. He stared, committing this moment to memory. Seven seconds flat. Good enough to put him in first place.

Ty didn't celebrate. Not yet. Garth Maitland still had to go. And while seven seconds flat was a damn fine time, Garth had beaten it before and could again today.

Stick appeared on the other side of the gate. "That was sure a nice run, Ty."

"Not bad."

"Want me to take Hamm for you?" Stick didn't add, "So you can stay and watch the rest of the competition." He didn't have to.

"Appreciate that."

After the teen left with the horse, Ty climbed onto the fence. He picked a spot away from the other competitors. If Garth beat him, he wanted a few minutes to himself before facing his friends.

But that wasn't going to happen. Not after the great run he'd had today.

The next contestant, a young man from Ecuador, finished at thirteen-point-three seconds. Ty hadn't been worried. The contestant after that had the potential to bump Ty out of the first place standing if he pulled off a miracle. But he didn't. The calf got loose at the last second, disqualifying him.

That left only Garth.

He was riding his regular horse and had been all weekend. The Buffalo Bill Cody Stampede might not be the biggest rodeo on the Turquoise Circuit, but he still wouldn't take a chance on a new horse.

"Folks, this cowboy needs a time of six-point-nine seconds to take over first place." The announcer's voice blared from the speakers overhead. "If anyone can do it, Garth Maitland sure can."

That was no lie.

Ty turned away from the box where Garth was going through his final equipment check, and scanned the crowd. He knew where the students from Cowboy College were sitting, and sought out Adele. At this distance it was impossible to see her face clearly. Even so, he was certain she was looking at him and not Garth.

The sound of the chute opening had Ty snapping his attention back to the box.

He willed Garth to have a good run. Not

that Ty didn't want to win. But he wanted a victory because he'd earned it, not because his biggest rival performed poorly.

The calf darted toward the far end of the arena. Every movement Garth and his horse made was straight out of a textbook. Running along the rope his mount held taut, he dropped the calf to the ground and tied its legs.

The crowd roared, their applause and cheers drowning out the announcer.

Ty didn't need to hear. His gut told him the run was a good one. Better than good, it was great. Equal to his own.

But was it better?

"Ladies and gentlemen, bear with us," the announcer's voice declared. "This is close, and the officials need to be one hundred percent sure."

Ty caught sight of Garth as he reached the gate. Their gazes connected, and Garth gave the briefest of nods. Ty returned it, his silent message the same.

Good run, cowboy.

"Hold on to your hats, folks, we have it," the announcer proclaimed. "Garth Maitland's official time is seven-point-three seconds. That makes Ty Boudeau your winner today!" Cheers exploded from the stands. "With Garth Maitland in second place and Ricky Morales in third."

Ty closed his eyes and dropped his head, savoring the moment. He'd won before, plenty of times. But no victory had ever been sweeter or more hard earned. He was, he knew now without a doubt, on his way to the top. This time he wouldn't lose at the National Finals Rodeo. He and Hamm would take home the title of World Champion and a generous sponsorship deal with it.

All at once, he was surrounded. Friends and fellow contestants pulled him off the fence, congratulating him and slapping him on the back.

"Hell of a run, Ty."

"You had me scared there for a minute, buddy, but you pulled it off."

He took it all in, his grin stretched so wide his face hurt.

"I knew you could do it." Pop appeared beside him.

"I couldn't have without your and Adele's help. I owe the both of you." Ty pulled the older man into a hug. More backslapping followed, for both him and Pop.

"Maybe I should sign up for a week at Cowboy College," a young man said jokingly.

"Maybe you should," Mitch Benson answered, his face serious.

Ty didn't think that was such a bad idea.

The speakers crackled to life again, and the announcer's voice carried across the arena. "The day's not over yet, folks. Stay in your seats, 'cause next up is the event you've been waiting for. Bull riding."

"See you in Sheridan?" Mitch asked.

Ty shook the hand he extended. "I'll be there. And having another run like today."

"I'm counting on it."

Eventually, everyone started clearing away. Some returned to their trailers to pack up, done for the weekend. Others took a place on the fence or in the bleachers to watch the bull riding.

Ty and Pop hadn't gone more than a few steps when Garth appeared in front of them.

"Congratulations," he told Ty.

"You didn't do so bad yourself today."

"First in team roping. I guess I can live with that."

"Enjoy it while it lasts. I plan on entering team roping at Sheridan."

Pop clapped Ty on the shoulder. "I'll catch

up with you later, son. Garth, give your family my regards."

After Pop left, Garth asked, "Who's your partner?"

"I'm not sure yet." Louis had informed Ty earlier that he wouldn't be going to Sheridan.

"How 'bout me?"

Ty laughed. "You're not serious."

"As a heart attack. Willie's kids are getting older, and his wife doesn't want him to go on the road anymore."

Ty understood. "Team rope with you?" he repeated, surprised at how much the idea appealed to him.

"Why not?"

Why not indeed.

"I guess we could give it a try. See how we work together."

Garth grinned. "How long until you leave Seven Cedars?"

He'd been planning on leaving mid-week. Now, he wasn't so sure. "Not for a few days."

"Why don't you come by Tuesday morning? We'll give it a go."

"I'll be there."

"Seven o'clock. Main arena."

No sooner did Garth walk away, than Adele appeared. Ty had no idea how long she'd been standing there or what she'd heard. Only that he couldn't be happier to see her, or wait any longer to hold her.

"You won." She smiled shyly.

"I did." He took a step toward her. "Now, about our date—"

"There he is!"

"Whoo, hoo! Ty, you were amazing."

All at once, he was surrounded by Mike and Sandy and the other students from Cowboy College. Enduring more backslapping, handshakes and hugs, he craned his neck to catch sight of Adele. Good. She hadn't left.

"We're having a celebration potluck cookout tonight at Pop's camper." Sandy's eyes pleaded with Ty. "Say you'll be there."

"Well, I…"

"I know you're probably going out with the other contestants." Her face fell. "But please come. Just for a little while."

"Don't pressure the man," Mike admonished.

Just beyond the group, Adele smiled coyly, obviously amused.

Ty pushed back his hat. "I guess I can come for a while."

Sandy threw her arms around him.

"You'll be there, too, won't you?" one of the students asked Adele.

Her gaze, soft and warm and hinting at what the night might bring, landed on Ty.

He drew in a sharp breath.

"I wouldn't miss it for the world," she said.

Neither would he.

Adele surveyed the area beside her grandfather's truck. If not for the absence of a flickering fire and nocturnal creatures calling to each other, the setting for their gathering could have been a cookout in the woods by Little Twister Creek.

Lawn chairs and overturned crates had been set up in a circle around the portable grill, enhancing the simple but hearty meal they all shared and the conversation that flowed easily—most of it centered on Ty. Kerosene lanterns atop folding tables attracted moths, while alternately casting shadows and light on people's faces.

Ty sat at the head of the circle, relishing the moment. Well, he deserved it, thought Adele. It wasn't easy coming back from a crushing defeat like the one he'd endured. She'd been proud of him today, admiring his tenacity and drive.

Then again, there were a number of things she admired about Ty, including the natural camaraderie he had with people, drawing them to him like those lanterns did the insects. He'd known most of the students here tonight only a short time, yet he treated them like old friends, and they him. It was no surprise Iron Grip Ropes had approached him about a sponsorship deal last year. He'd have made a perfect spokesman. If he continued winning, which he would, maybe they'd approach him again.

Building custom-made saddles the quality of Charlie Kingston's was a fine occupation, but Adele couldn't help thinking Ty was better suited to doing something that got him out and about, rather than being stuck in a workroom all day.

Well, she doubted he'd be building saddles full-time for a while. Not until he retired from rodeoing, which, now that he'd discovered the previously missing connection with Hamm, wouldn't be for several years at least.

Adele went around collecting trash and depositing it in a plastic garbage bag. Some of their neighbors had already packed up their trailers and RVs and departed, leaving open spaces in the makeshift gypsy camp. Most were like her and Pop, planning to start out for home at the crack of dawn.

Pop, in his element, stole the spotlight from Ty and regaled the students with stories from back in the day when he'd competed. Everyone, including Ty, listened raptly.

Despite having had an emotional day with highs, lows and moments of downright confusion, Adele felt a sense of satisfaction. This pleasant gathering of friends, guests and people she cared about was the kind she'd envisioned when she and her grandfather first started Cowboy College.

Not that there weren't sacrifices. She had few opportunities to travel and see the country as she longed to, given all the responsibilities she shouldered.

Yet another reason she and Ty were a poor match. He would settle down eventually. In the meantime, however, he'd be going wherever his rodeo career took him, and that would be miles and miles away from Markton, Wyoming.

"Need help with that?" Sandy asked. Their potluck dinner had consisted mostly of leftovers, topped off with ice cream and peach pies someone had purchased earlier at the market down the road.

"I'm fine," Adele said. "You go sit yourself back down."

Sandy paused, her arms crossed, and stared at the group. "I'm going to miss all this."

"We'll miss you, too."

"Tomorrow when we check out, Mike and I are going to make reservations for next summer."

"That's great. We'd love to have you back."

"We want to come at the same time Ty does."

Adele paused in the middle of securing the garbage bag with a twist tie. "I...don't think he's coming back," she said carefully.

"No?" Sandy appeared puzzled. "He said he was."

"When?"

"Just a little bit ago."

"He did?"

Adele must have given herself away, for Sandy laughed richly. "I thought that might make you happy."

"Of course it does. It's our goal for all our guests to return."

"But Ty in particular."

No, what she really wanted was for Ty to stay and not leave.

But he would. Especially after winning the

gold buckle today. That was the whole reason he'd come to Cowboy College. To figure out what he'd been doing wrong, fix it, return to the circuit as soon as possible and resume his promising career.

"*You and Mike* in particular," Adele emphasized, trying to cover her slip.

"Hey, we all think it's great that you and Ty hooked up."

We all? As in the entire guest roster? Adele waited for mortification to overcome her— only it didn't. To her shock, she realized she wasn't upset that guests, and no doubt staff, too, knew she and Ty had "hooked up," as Sandy put it.

"We will see you before we leave, won't we?"

Sandy's question roused Adele from her reverie. "Of course. We'll have a goodbye party at lunch."

"What's that about a party?" Mike asked, coming up and giving his wife's waist a squeeze.

"Adele said we're having one at lunch tomorrow."

"Can I come, too?"

At the sound of Ty's voice behind her, Adele went still.

"Of course." Conscious of her audience,

she set the bag of trash by the truck door for disposal later. "Everyone's invited."

"Sandy and I were thinking of going to the country and western bar up the road for something stronger than this." Mike held out his plastic bottle of iced tea. "Some of the folks were saying the band's not half-bad. You two want to go?"

"It's not a far walk," Sandy prompted.

"I don't know." Ty sent Adele a questioning look.

Technically, they had a date tonight, payment for him winning his event. If he wanted to go to the bar, she'd gladly accompany him.

The gleam in his dark eyes, coal-black in the lantern light, indicated he was thinking of something more than a few close dances and a searing kiss or two under a star-filled sky.

Was she ready for that and all the complications that went with it?

If not, she had better tell him no right now.

"Be back in a while, Pop," she called out, without looking away from Ty.

"Stay out of trouble, you two," he hollered back, an unmistakable smile in his voice.

Define trouble, Adele thought as Ty fell into step beside her.

Chapter 11

Sandy's mile-a-minute chatter hid the fact that Ty and Adele contributed very little to the conversation. Adele couldn't speak for him, but in her case, an acute case of nerves had frozen her vocal cords. Instinct told her whatever happened tonight between them would be entirely up to her. He would respect and honor any decision she made.

If only she was certain what her decision would be.

Correction.

If only she was certain she wouldn't end up being hurt.

Sandy's prattling continued as they reached the outskirts of the makeshift gypsy camp.

"Hold on." Ty stopped in midstep and patted his jeans pocket. "I forgot my wallet in my trailer."

"We'll walk back with you," Mike offered.

"I hate to hold you up."

"You sure?" Sandy asked, her oval face lit by the parking lot lights.

"Go on ahead and find us a table."

They started out, then stopped again. "You coming?" Mike asked Adele.

Her vocal cords had yet to thaw.

"Come on." Sandy linked arms with her husband. "They'll be along in a minute." Dragging him with her, she glanced over her shoulder and chimed, "Take your time, you two."

"My trailer's this way." Ty inclined his head in the direction they'd come.

Adele nodded, swallowed and took a step.

He reached for her hand. When it was clasped firmly in his, walking wasn't nearly so difficult.

"I didn't plan this," he said, his voice low and husky. "I really did forget my wallet."

She believed him. Cowboys didn't usually carry their wallets when they competed, and

Ty hadn't returned to his trailer since winning his event.

They saw many familiar faces as they navigated among the campsites. If their joined hands solicited any attention, Adele didn't care. As Sandy had pointed out, everyone at Cowboy College knew about her and Ty's attraction. So what if the rest of the world found out, too?

Suddenly, Adele wasn't indecisive anymore. Her heart, which had been whispering to her softly for weeks, now spoke loud and clear, urging her to seize the moment.

"I'm parked over there."

She followed his gaze. Ty's trailer stood alone, his neighbors having left already. Hamm, along with the other horses, was bedded down in the event stables.

Going straight to the rear wheel well, Ty located a hidden key and unlocked the side door, careful not to let it bang against the wall. At this time of night, the noise would carry half a mile.

"I won't be long," he said, and reached through the open door.

A dim light came on, illuminating the postage-stamp-size living quarters. Placing an old footstool on the ground, he grabbed the side-mounted handhold and easily hefted himself up and inside the trailer.

Adele heard the scrape of a sliding drawer. The scuffle of boots on linoleum flooring. The jingle of keys being dropped on the counter. She also heard the sound of her own boots on the footstool as she copied Ty and clasped the handhold.

He turned, his expression unreadable as he took in the sight of her standing in the trailer doorway. "The place is a little small, but I'd be happy to show you around."

Was he keeping his emotions in check? Making a joke in case he'd misinterpreted the reason she'd so boldly entered his private space? A space that could be even more private if the door was shut. Reaching behind her, she swung it closed. The clicking latch echoed loudly in the suddenly quiet interior.

So did the beating of her soaring heart.

"Adele?"

She hadn't spoken since leaving Pop's campsite, and didn't now.

Crossing the small distance separating them, she reached up and circled his neck with her arms. His eyes, which had tracked her progress, instantly went from unreadable to blazing hot.

"You know this is dangerous," he said in a roughened voice, pulling her close until their bodies were flush and their hips aligned.

Was it? Adele had been thinking it was exciting and daring and incredibly intoxicating. Not dangerous.

She sought his mouth, moaning softly at the first touch of his lips. Moaning again when the kiss became possessive. Heat arrowed though her, igniting every nerve in its path. This, she thought numbly, was only the beginning. There could—and would—be so much more.

Ty pushed away from her, catching her off guard, his chest heaving. "We'd better slow it down some."

Adele made a sound of protest.

"I can't take much more of this and stay sane."

They'd have to risk his sanity, she thought, a smile pulling at her lips. She liked the hard ridge of his erection pressing firmly into the junction of her legs—liked it too much to stop.

Nestling closer, she rubbed her calf along his and twirled her fingers in the soft curls at the back of his neck.

As if in surrender, he leaned against the closet door behind him. "Adele, sweetheart. Please."

Please what? Leave him alone or give in to the desire that had been building practically since the day he arrived at Cowboy College?

She laid her palms flat on his chest. Beneath the fabric of his shirt, his heart beat fast and erratically. How much of it, she wondered, had he given to her? Enough that it would be torture for him to leave her in a few days?

Yes. She didn't require a declaration made on bended knee to know she'd come to mean something special to him. Something he wouldn't find anywhere else, regardless of where his travels took him.

She brought her hands together over the top button of his shirt and quickly unfastened it.

Before she got to the second button, he grasped her wrist, staying her motions. "Are you sure?"

Nodding, she gazed at him, hoping he saw the depths of her feelings for him reflected in her face.

"Say something, Adele. Please."

She put him out of his misery. "Make love to me, Ty."

She expected him to respond with another kiss, one designed to rob her of her ability to think coherently. He didn't. Instead, he tucked her head snugly against his chest and brushed his lips across her hair.

"I want you to know this won't be a casual fling."

Could it be anything else? He was leaving soon.

"I'll be back for you. Count on it."

His earnestness touched her.

"I'll be waiting," she said.

He kissed her then, sweetly, tenderly and with a gentleness she wouldn't have expected from a rugged, brawny cowboy like him.

Quickly, however, the kiss turned scorching. His mouth, unsatisfied with teasing and tormenting just her lips, sought out other sensitive places on her body. Her neck. The delicate skin of her earlobe. The soft hollow at the base of her throat.

Adele's limbs went weak as a needy moan escaped.

All at once Ty was tugging at her shirttail, releasing it from the waistband of her jeans. Then he reached up under the fabric and grasped her waist.

Opening his shirt, she ran her hands down his white cotton T-shirt, enjoying the sensation of downy fabric over the taut planes of his chest. All during their sensual interplay, his lips continued exploring her sensitive regions. That stopped when her fingers brushed against his belt buckle. With a deep groan, he claimed her mouth again, stripping her shirt from her as he did.

The lighting was dim, but Ty still had a clear view of her baby-blue bra. He traced a fingertip along the lacy trim, murmuring, "Nice."

And it was. Adele might be all cowgirl on the outside, but she had an appreciation for delicate underthings.

"You told me to wear something sexy."

Emboldened by his hungry gaze, she peeled his shirt from his shoulders. He took over, shrugging it off and removing his T-shirt. She'd expected him to have a well-honed body, considering how hard he worked at roping, and she wasn't disappointed.

All at once she saw it, a lasso tattoo circling his upper right arm. It fit Ty's personality and brought a smile to her lips. "Nice," she murmured, echoing his earlier remark.

"You don't mind tattoos?"

"I have one, too."

His eyes lit up. "Where?"

She lowered the strap of her bra, revealing a tiny horse's head with flowing mane above her left breast. The same one used in the Cowboy College logo.

Ty's breath caught. Lowering his mouth, he pressed his lips to the tattoo.

Even if Adele had wanted to guard her emotions, she couldn't any longer. Not after this. Not with Ty.

She gasped when he unexpectedly tugged down the front of her bra and cupped her freed breast. Gasped again when he circled the nipple with his tongue.

In a hurry, she grabbed at her own belt.

Ty raised his head. "No rush, sweetheart. We've got all night. Unless you still want to go to the bar with Mike and Sandy."

"Not on your life." She finished unbuckling her belt, then attacked the snap on her jeans.

"Wait." Ty covered her hands with his.

"What?"

Before her insecurities could get the better of her, he said, "I…have protection." He fumbled for the wallet on the counter, opened it and withdrew a condom.

"That's good." Stupid her. She'd been so caught up in making love with Ty, she'd forgotten about being responsible.

"I want you to know…" Again he hesitated. "This has been in my wallet awhile." He tried to grin. "In case you thought otherwise."

There were cowboys on the rodeo circuit notorious for sleeping around. And they had plenty of obliging women at their disposal. Adele believed Ty, however, and not just because he had a reputation for being one of the honorable guys. She believed him because of the genuine worry in his expression.

"I didn't think otherwise," she said. "And for the record, it's been a long while for me, too."

"Glad that's settled," he said, and kissed her again.

With all doubts erased and all barriers eradicated, they were able to revel in the feel of each other's body and the wildly erotic sensations generated by their intimate explorations. The tiny living quarters didn't allow much space for maneuvering. And without stopping to convert the dining table into a sleeping bunk, they had nowhere to lie down.

Ty showed himself to be good at improvising.

Removing the remainder of Adele's clothing, he lifted her onto the table. When she reached for him, he grabbed a pillow from the seat, placed it behind her and lowered her backward.

Starting at the horse's head tattoo, he traveled the length of her body to the V of her legs, leaving moist kisses in his wake. The skill of his mouth was matched only by the skill of his fingers. Both tantalized her unmercifully, and within minutes, she was perched on the pinnacle of release.

He didn't, however, take her over the edge, and she almost cried out in frustration when he straightened. All was forgiven when he unbuckled his jeans and stepped out of them.

She raised up on her elbows, to better see Ty in his slim fitting boxer briefs. Without the least bit of modesty, he removed them, opened the condom package and sheathed himself. Pulse soaring, she sat upright, every nerve alight with anticipation.

Except he didn't move.

"Ty? What's wrong?"

"Nothing." His dark eyes studied her from head to toe. "I just like looking at you."

He certainly knew how to prolong the agony. Or was that pleasure? Definitely pleasure. Her entire body hummed with it.

Unable to wait any longer, she arched her spine and smiled temptingly.

That did it. With an agonized groan, he grasped her legs and anchored her to him.

Adele gasped in surprise, then delight, when he entered her. Wrapping her legs around his middle, she clung to him, wanting an emotional connection with him more than she did a physical one.

Ty held back, she could tell. And as much as she wanted to tumble over the edge, she also wanted their lovemaking to last.

Murmuring sweet, sexy endearments, he bent her backward until she once again lay on the table. Covering her with his body, he kissed her deeply, his hands cupping her breasts.

Adele could wait no longer and climaxed, Ty's name on her lips. He found his own shattering release seconds later.

She clung tightly to him, savoring the aftermath of their shared storm almost as much as she had the storm itself.

Slowly, their breathing returned to normal. What could have been an awkward moment was made comfortable and easy when Ty lifted her off the table and enveloped her in a warm embrace.

"That was amazing," he said, caressing her back with strong strokes. "You're amazing."

Adele turned her face into the side of his neck. She hardly considered herself an accomplished lover. Yet it *had* been amazing with Ty. More than that, it had felt…perfect.

For a moment, she imagined them together always.

Then, too soon, reality returned.

* * *

"I suppose we should get to the bar," Adele said, easing away from Ty to look for her clothes. "Mike and Sandy are expecting us."

"Do you really want to go?"

She shook her head. "But I'm not sure I want to stand here all night. Naked, at that."

One corner of his mouth tilted up in a wicked grin. "The table converts to a bed."

She liked that idea.

Laughing together, they hurriedly removed the tabletop and replaced it with a plank, then arranged the cushions into a mattress. Ty pulled a worn sleeping bag from the overhead cupboard, and they cuddled beneath it, his arm draped over her protectively and their fingers linked.

"Come with me to Ogden," he said out of the blue.

"Utah?"

"The Pioneer Days Rodeo starts the third weekend in July."

"That's only two weeks away."

"Plenty of time to pack."

"I'd love to go with you." She rolled over to face him. "More than you know. But I have to work. I can't just up and leave, not on such short notice."

"There's no one to cover for you?"

"It's our busy season."

"Then I'll skip Ogden."

"No, you won't." She pressed a light kiss to his lips. "You're winning again. You have to ride the momentum all the way to Nationals."

"I'm winning because of you."

"You always had the ability. I just helped you realize it."

"I'm coming back to Seven Cedars." He moved suddenly, throwing a leg over her and pinning her to the cushions. His hand boldly roamed her buttocks and thighs. "Don't think I'm not."

She arched into him. "I'll be waiting."

"Promise me."

A vulnerability she hadn't seen before shone in his eyes.

"I promise." The vow came easily.

"I know long-distance relationships are difficult, but we can make this work. There isn't anything I want more."

Hearing his conviction, she almost believed they could succeed where her parents had failed. Ty spent the next hour convincing her, with actions that left no doubt as to his sincerity.

* * *

Hamm entered the horse trailer without his customary balking, as if he couldn't wait to leave Cowboy College and Seven Cedars Ranch.

Adele would have preferred he put up a fight.

She'd been dreading this moment for the last five days, ever since the night she and Ty had spent together in his trailer. Standing off to the side, she watched him shut the trailer door, latch and lock it, then check the lock again just to make sure. Was he really worried that the door would swing open during the drive or simply delaying their final goodbye? He'd already missed his planned 9:00 A.M. departure time by almost an hour.

If anyone had noticed she'd spent the last four nights in Ty's cabin rather than her apartment, they said nothing. Probably because they approved of her and Ty's relationship, albeit for different reasons. Pop had more than once vocalized his desire to see Adele settled, and the employees were, she suspected, glad their boss was enjoying something other than work for a change. Reese had openly expressed her joy during Ty and Garth's first official team roping practice on Tuesday. But then, she was happily engaged to be married, and wanted all her friends to be happy, too.

"You drive careful, you hear?" Cook said. She was among the small crowd that had gathered to see Ty off.

"You're welcome back anytime." Pop's voice had a slight catch in it.

So, Adele thought, did Ty's when he answered. "I'm taking you up on that offer."

The two men started out shaking hands, but Ty pulled Pop into a bear hug. Adele felt her throat close. Five days of mental preparation obviously wasn't enough. She couldn't remember the last time she'd done anything half this hard.

"Stick, I'm counting on you to watch out for Adele and Pop while I'm gone." Ty hooked an arm around the skinny teenager's neck.

"Sure thing."

"You're a good man."

Stick's perpetual goofy grin widened.

Ty spoke to each person there, dispensing handshakes, hugs and pecks on cheeks, including one for Lani. Adele and she were on better terms, thanks in large part to Pop's recent revelations, but Adele continued to be guarded around her, unconvinced her mother had changed her ways.

Watching Lani hug Ty, Adele thought she

saw genuine tears well in her mother's eyes, and she was struck with a sentimental pang. The next moment, she dismissed it. Lani knew how to put on an act with the best of them, especially around men.

Tipping his hat in one last farewell to all, Ty went to Adele and took her hand. "Walk me to my truck."

Though she generally shied away from public displays of affection, no way was he leaving without a last, lingering kiss.

Ty was of the same mind, except he carried it one step further. Amid good-natured hoots and hollers, he bent her over his arm and planted a kiss on her mouth to beat all kisses. Adele's toes were still tingling when he released her.

"I'll call you tonight."

She nodded, afraid she might cry if she tried to talk.

He reached for the door handle.

"Wait!"

Throwing her arms around him, she stood on tiptoes and pressed her face into the curve of his neck. "I'll miss you."

"Me, too, sweetheart."

Two minutes later, he was gone, his truck and trailer pulling out of the open area and heading down the long drive that would take him past the main lodge and to the highway beyond.

Adele stood there watching until the last plume of dust had dissipated. During her vigil, the others left, perhaps sensing her need to be alone.

Not yet ready to return to work, she strolled to the small barn. It had been several days since her last visit with Crackers. More than that, the quiet solitude would enable her to fortify her defenses before having to deal with people and the inevitable well-intentioned platitudes or personal questions.

Crackers nickered hello. The filly—Adele had named her Ritz—pushed her nose up, seeking a petting. Naturally curious and playful, Ritz couldn't get enough attention.

It was exactly the balm Adele needed to soothe her aching heart. She'd done her best to resist Ty, and yet she'd fallen for him. Head over heels and faster than she'd ever imagined possible. The three weeks until he returned were going to seem like three decades.

"There you are!"

Adele winced. *Oh, no! Why now?*

"I'm glad I found you." Lani scurried toward her, a big, bright smile on her face.

"Hi, Mom. I was just about to get ready for class." Yes, it was a lie, but Adele felt she'd be forgiven this once.

"There's something I need to tell you." Lani

came to a stop, looking chagrined. The expression took several years off her face, transforming her into the attractive woman she'd once been. Adele also noticed her mother had filled out a little recently, the extra weight adding a softness to her previous bone-thin frame. "I've been stalling and stalling, and I just can't anymore."

She's leaving! Adele had been anticipating just such an announcement for weeks.

"I'm moving." Lani's smile reappeared.

"Where to?" Adele didn't add, "this time."

"Right in town. I found an efficiency apartment to rent. It's not much, but will do for a while. I need to get my own place and stop mooching off you and your grandfather."

"Oh." When did her mother start worrying about being a mooch?

"And it's close to the feed store."

Adele's stomach dropped to her knees. She should have guessed Lani wanted her own place nearby in order to carry on her affair with Henry.

"He's a married man, Mom."

"Who?"

"Henry."

"I know that."

"And it doesn't stop you?"

"From what?" Lani shook her head in confusion.

"Sleeping with him," Adele all but spit out.

"Good heavens! Is that what you think?"

"I saw you and him at the Spotted Horse."

Hurt—and disappointment?—glinted in Lani's eyes. "He offered me a job."

"A job?"

"At the feed store. His assistant manager gave notice." Lani sniffed. "I don't take up with married men. And I certainly don't take up with my boss."

"I—I…" Adele was speechless.

"I thought if I got a full-time job and my own place, that maybe you and I could, well, work things out. I've made a ton of mistakes over the years and was just trying to fix a few of them." She sniffed again. "I guess I was wrong."

"Mom." Adele struggled to find the words—any words—to say. "I'm sorry. I jumped to the wrong conclusion."

Lani's face crumpled. "I'm sorry, too. I really did want to do the right thing for once. And when Henry offered me the job, I figured it was a good place to start."

A job and an apartment. One Lani paid for herself. Not an affair. And a chance to repair some of those burned bridges. Small steps in a very right direction.

Part of Adele resisted. Lani had never been much of a mother, disappointing her one too many times for her to be sucked in by the promise of change.

But if she didn't acknowledge her mom's efforts and support them, then perhaps she wasn't much of a daughter, either.

"It is a good place to start. I'm glad for you."

"Really?" Lani's teary eyes shone.

"And…proud."

"Oh, baby." Lani pulled her into a fierce hug. "I'm so proud of you, too. Everything you've done, the ranch, Cowboy College. Much as I tried to screw you up, you still turned out to be this incredible woman. Smart and talented and…oh, that Ty Boudeau is one lucky fellow to have you."

Slowly, very slowly, Adele returned her mother's hug. After a moment, she increased the pressure.

Maybe it was having a wonderful man like Ty in her life. Maybe it was being secure at Seven Cedars and knowing her place in the world. Whatever the reason, Adele felt some of the resentment she'd carried around for over twenty years fade, and her spirits, which had sunk so low when Ty left, gradually lift.

Chapter 12

All Ty wanted, all he'd been thinking about for the last eight hours and the last four hundred miles, was seeing Adele. Holding her, kissing her, unraveling that long braid of hers and running his fingers through her silky hair. Seven phone calls, starting this morning and ending just outside of Markton, hadn't slaked his desire to see her. If anything, they'd increased it.

The sight of the main gate leading into Seven Cedars hit Ty like a drink of cool water after a long walk in the hot desert.

He was home.

Wait a minute! When had he started thinking of Seven Cedars as home?

Since he'd left three weeks ago. Not an hour passed when he didn't imagine returning to Adele and everything he'd come to hold dear.

His gaze scanned right and left as his truck bumped along the drive and into the open area in front of the barns. He was early, but had hoped Adele would be waiting for him. They'd agreed during one of those seven phone calls that he would take Hamm to the small corral east of the arena and let him run around a bit before putting him up for the night.

A night Ty intended to spend every moment of, waking and sleeping, with Adele.

Hamm, impatient as always to be free, banged a foot on the trailer door the instant the truck came to a stop. Three minutes later, the big gelding was trotting off steam, tossing his head, and strutting his stuff for the other horses in the nearby pasture.

Ty took out his cell phone, intending to call Adele.

"He looks happy to be out."

He spun at the sound of Pop's voice behind him, and grinned broadly. "He's not the only one."

"Long drive?"

"Too long. My legs are killing me."

"How about I trade you for mine?"

Ty had noticed the older man's limp was more pronounced than before. "Hip bothering you?"

"Some. But not, I hope, for long."

"I heard you finally agreed to the replacement surgery."

Adele had given Ty the news the day after he left. It seemed Pop had postponed telling her so as not to interfere with her and Ty's time together.

"A week from Thursday," Pop said. "I wanted to wait, but that granddaughter of mine is a hard one to resist."

Ty concurred wholeheartedly.

"She's in her office if you're looking for her."

"I don't want to disturb her if she's working."

"I'm thinking she won't mind."

"Hamm needs to—"

"Go on. I'll take care of your horse."

"You sure?"

Pop scowled. "I'm not a cripple yet."

Ty needed no further persuading.

As he walked across the lobby's hardwood floor, he was reminded of his first day at the ranch and of how much had changed during the last seven weeks. He and Hamm were in perfect sync, with three shiny new buckles to show for it. Two in tie-down roping and one in team roping with Garth. That didn't count the two second-place finishes Ty had taken in steer wrestling. Altogether, the winnings were enough to bankroll him for the next six rodeos, as well as make a small but overdue payment to his parents.

And then there was Adele. He hated being apart from her, but knowing that what he was doing would eventually give them the means for a life together fueled his determination and made the long, lonely days without her bearable.

He hurried his steps, their echo resounding through the empty lobby. She must have heard him, for she appeared in the office doorway just as he was rounding the registration counter.

"You're early," she said, her face alight with excitement.

"I broke enough traffic laws to put me away for years if I'd been caught."

"I'm glad you weren't."

Not caring if anyone walked by and saw them, he clasped her in his arms. The next instant, his mouth was where it had wanted to be for hours. Days. Weeks. And he didn't hurry, despite them having only until the morning before he had to leave again for the next rodeo. This moment was worth savoring.

Except Adele had other ideas.

She didn't merely return his kiss, she took control of it, giving him a hint of what to expect later.

"That's some greeting," he said, his entire body responding to the fire in her eyes and the heat in her touch. "Mind if I leave and come back for another one?"

"Don't worry, cowboy. There's more where that came from."

He laughed, his first real one in weeks. Did she have any idea how good she made him feel? "I've missed you."

Her features abruptly crumbled, and she shielded her face with her hand.

"You're not crying, are you?"

"No." But she was.

Ty escorted her into her office, shutting the door behind them. "What's wrong, sweetheart?"

She wiped her cheek with the back of her hand. "I'm just happy to see you."

He sat down in her desk chair, then pulled her onto his lap. The chair groaned under their combined weight. "I'm happy to see you, too."

She curled into a ball, combing her fingers through his hair while he stroked her back.

"This isn't how I wanted it to be," she murmured. "I had other plans."

"From what I could tell earlier, I like your plans."

She tilted her face up to his, and he kissed her again. This time tenderly. "I don't know what's wrong with me lately. I've been so emotional."

"You have a lot going on. Pop said his surgery's next Thursday."

"Yeah. And while I can't wait for him to have it, I'm not looking forward to it." She outlined some of the details of the procedure and the daunting challenges she and her grandfather faced.

"Pop will do fine. He's not about to let a little thing like hip-replacement surgery get him down."

"You're right. I'm just not sure about me."

She nestled closer with a soft sigh. "Are you hungry yet?"

"Yes." Ty lowered his head and nibbled her ear.

She wriggled away. "I meant for food. We can have an early dinner in the dining hall and then…" She ended the sentence with an inviting smile.

"Or we could 'then' first, and have a late dinner."

He'd been joking—sort of. Adele surprised and delighted him by agreeing.

After stopping briefly to check on Hamm, they sneaked off to her apartment. Or tried to. Every few minutes they ran into someone glad to see Ty and wanting to chat. A half hour later they were finally alone, secluded in Adele's bedroom and tearing off each other's clothes.

When Adele would have hurried, Ty restrained her, determined to prolong the enjoyment. Afterward, they lay with their limbs entwined in her antique brass bed, her lavender sheets strewn across their bodies, the last rays of sunlight streaming through the parted curtains of her window.

"I talked to Garth yesterday," he said, his lips brushing the soft tendrils at her temple.

"Mmm?"

"His parents and Reese are flying out to the Steamboat Springs Rodeo this weekend. They've invited you to come along."

She shook her head. "I can't."

The conversation sounded a lot like their previous one. Regardless, Ty continued. "Why not? You'd only be gone three days."

"Pop's having his surgery."

"Next Thursday. You'll be back in plenty of time."

Adele shifted. Only a little, but the two inches felt like two feet.

"There are tests he has to have. Blood work, X-rays, consultations with the doctors. The medical center's a two-hour round trip. He can't drive it alone."

"Stick could go with him."

"But he can't help Pop with all the paperwork. And believe me, between the doctor, hospital and insurance company, there's a mountain of it. On top of that, I have to meet with the barn manager and the head wrangler. Make sure Pop's work is covered while he recuperates."

Ty felt overwhelmed just listening to her, and wished there was more he could do for her.

"I'm sorry." He pulled her against him,

not satisfied until those two inches separating them were reduced to a hair's width. "I'm pressuring you, and that's not my intention."

"I really wish I could come."

"Maybe I'll skip Steamboat Springs. Spend a few extra days here."

She immediately sat up and said sternly, "You'll do no such thing."

"I don't have to compete in every rodeo between now and Nationals."

"Have you qualified yet?"

"No, but—"

"Paid back your parents?"

"Not everything."

"Seriously, Ty." She groaned with exasperation. "You know better than anyone that things happen. Unexpected things. You've come too far and worked too hard to risk not qualifying."

She was right, though a part of him wished she wasn't.

"I guess we'll just have to make the most of this visit." He reached under the sheet, seeking and finding the smooth curve of her hip.

Her sigh of contentment turned into a moan of pleasure when he parted her legs.

The ring of her cell phone couldn't have come at a worse time.

"Don't answer it," he murmured, lowering his mouth to her breast.

"That's Pop's ring tone. If I don't pick up, he'll come looking for us."

Ty would have preferred weighing their options. Not Adele. She swung her legs over the side of the bed and rummaged around on the floor for her jeans.

"Yeah, Pop." She listened a moment, then held the phone away from her mouth. "Cook's putting together a little celebration dinner for you."

"Sounds like I can't say no."

"Wise man."

He lay in bed, both pillows stuffed under his head, watching her dress.

"Come on," she urged. "We're going to be late."

"I'd rather stay here with you."

She tugged on his arm. "It's only temporary."

Was it? He and Adele hadn't spoken about the future, not specifically and not beyond Nationals this winter. He suspected that, like him, she was thinking long term.

She'd *better* be thinking long term, Ty amended as he finally rolled out of bed and reached for his clothes. Because he had zero intentions of letting her go. Now or ever.

"This way." Adele took two steps. When she heard nothing, she stopped and glanced anxiously over her shoulder. "Easy now."

"I'm all right," Pop snapped. He'd caught one front wheel of his walker on the threshold leading from the garage to the kitchen.

She resisted hurrying to his aid. He was too stubborn to accept her help even if she did. Besides, Stick stood right behind him. The teenager might be skinny, but he was strong, and more than capable of catching her grandfather if he teetered.

The wheel finally gave, hopping over the threshold, and he maneuvered the shiny red walker into the kitchen. His steps were hesitant, measured and stiff, burdened by the compression stockings he was required to wear.

Adele hurt just looking at him.

The doctor, nurses and physical therapist, however, had praised Pop's progress, stating repeatedly that he was doing well for a man his age.

A man his age!

Adele had begun to view her grandfather

through different eyes and didn't like what she saw. Though in good health, he was getting older and slowing down. More of the responsibility of running the ranch and Cowboy College would fall to her, and not just during his recovery.

She prayed the next few weeks would go easier than this last one had. Talks with Pop's doctor prior to the surgery hadn't prepared her for the sight of him lying in the hospital bed surrounded by tubes and monitors, a bulky dressing on his hip and his complexion the color of paste. Her emotions, riding so close to the surface of late, had overwhelmed her, causing tears to fall at the least little provocation.

Oddly enough, it had been her mother who was there for Adele the day of the surgery, sitting with her in the family waiting area. Lani also found time to make the long drive and visit Pop twice during his hospital stay, though she remained only briefly because of her work schedule.

It was Ty, however, who had provided the most support for Adele during and after Pop's surgery. He volunteered to fly in for a day or two, but she'd have none of it, insisting he stay and continue to ride his winning streak.

She'd have felt differently if Pop's surgery had been life threatening. Ty's phone calls, three a day at least, were enough for now. They gave her a break from the many nerve-racking demands placed on her, and reassured her that what they had together was special and important to him.

That didn't stop her from occasionally wondering if they'd be able to endure the continued long separations. When Ty mentioned her traveling with him on the circuit, or returning to Santa Fe to visit his parents, she allowed herself to get swept up in his excitement. Then she would look at her grandfather and accept the reality that she'd probably never travel any farther than the medical center in Cody. Not for a while, anyway.

Would Ty wait for her?

She hadn't yet found the courage to ask him.

All at once, a wave of nausea struck her. She sucked in a harsh breath and pressed a hand to her stomach. Just as quickly, the feeling subsided, and she exhaled with relief. The stress was getting to her. She'd been feeling mildly ill off and on since before Pop went in for his surgery. And tired. Some mornings, she barely had the energy to climb out of bed, requiring a second cup of coffee to get her day started. She'd be so glad when Pop got back on his feet.

"Did you remember my prescriptions from the car?" Pop stood in the middle of the kitchen, his chest rising and falling from the exertion. And all he'd done was walk from the car.

"Right here." Adele held up a small white sack.

"What about my overnight bag?"

"I'll get that later. Unless you need it this second."

"Guess not," he grumbled.

He wasn't being intentionally difficult, she knew. His doctor had warned Adele to expect periodic mood swings. In addition to the surgery taking a toll on him, there was the daunting prospect of being mostly house-bound for two to four weeks. Pop didn't do modified bed rest and restricted activity well.

"Come on, Pop," Stick said good-naturedly. "I'll help you to bed."

"All right, all right. Don't rush me."

"You want some lunch?" Adele asked.

"Not yet. Maybe later."

Her grandfather going willingly to bed and

not hungry? Her worry instantly flared. He must really feel awful.

"I'll take something, if you're offering." Stick grinned sheepishly.

"Coming right up."

While he settled her grandfather in bed, she threw a quick lunch together. The aroma of grilling cheese sandwiches started her stomach roiling again. Piling the one she'd fixed for herself on Stick's plate, she heated up a bowl of canned chicken-noodle soup, hoping that would sit better.

She was just putting the lunch on the table when Ty called her cell phone.

"How's Pop? You two get home okay?"

"A little bit ago." The sexy timbre of his voice warmed her from the inside out. No matter how often he called, she never grew tired of hearing it. Especially late at night.

Stick came down the hall, spied the lunch on the table and fell on it like a typical ravenous teenager.

"How's Pop?" Adele mouthed.

"Sleeping," Stick managed to say between bites.

"Stick's here, helping out," she told Ty.

"That's good. Hey, I was thinking of coming out on Monday for a couple days."

"Aren't you in Missoula?"

"Just pulled into the fairgrounds."

Missoula was a long way from Markton. "When do you compete?"

"I'll be done Sunday afternoon by five. I checked with the airlines and can catch a late flight. A friend of mine's agreed to take care of Hamm for me. Problem is, I wouldn't land until about 10:00 P.M. your time. Is that too late?"

Yellowstone Regional Airport was over a hundred miles away. Picking up Ty added yet another task to her already extensive list. Then driving him back two days later.

But, oh, she wanted to be with him. Sleep for ten hours straight wrapped in his arms. Okay, she admitted it. Sleep wasn't the only activity she had in mind. After showing him how happy she was to see him, they'd loll around in bed all morning, not rising until the sun was high in the sky.

No, they wouldn't. She'd have to come here and check on Pop. Make sure he was doing okay.

"I—I don't know," she stammered.

"I miss you."

His longing carried across the miles, and her heart melted. "I'll be there at ten sharp waiting for you."

If necessary, she'd hire a nurse for two days. Or see if one of the wranglers' wives was interested in earning a little extra money. Pop might be more receptive to that idea.

"Wear your blue bra," Ty said in a husky drawl.

She laughed and stepped into the family room, away from Stick's prying ears. He didn't need to hear the more private details of her conversation with Ty. Some minutes later, when they disconnected, she rationalized her decision to let him come by telling herself a visit from him would boost Pop's morale.

But it was her own morale that was now soaring in anticipation. So much so that she wolfed down her reheated soup and went back for seconds.

"Call if you need me," Stick said later, on his way out the door.

"I will." Adele hoped she wouldn't have to.

While Pop continued to nap, she tidied the kitchen and emptied the car. The four-door sedan belonged to Garth's parents. They'd been kind enough to lend it to Adele and Pop while he recovered, for which she was enormously grateful. She couldn't imagine trying to wrestle her grandfather in and out of his tall truck.

When she finished unloading, she went into the old master bedroom and unpacked her few belongings. They'd agreed she would reside with Pop until he could manage on his own. She hadn't brought much with her, figuring on returning to her apartment every day for whatever she needed.

Her grandparents' bedroom had remained virtually untouched for eight years, and Adele found herself studying pictures on the wall and knickknacks on the dresser that were still where her grandmother had placed them.

It would be strange spending the night here, sleeping among the memories.

A knock on the kitchen door had her hurrying down the hall in her stocking feet.

"Coming!" she called, then remembered her grandfather was sleeping.

Whoever had shown up was comfortable enough that they'd used the back door. Probably one of the hands checking on Pop, or someone from the kitchen. Adele had arranged with Cook to have meals delivered during his convalescence.

It was none of those people.

"Hey, baby girl."

"Mom! What are you doing here? I thought you were at work."

* * *

Adele stepped back so that her mother could come inside, silently chiding the part of her that wished Lani had called first and not just shown up.

"Henry let me off early today." Lani carried a plastic grocery sack bearing the name Bush's General Store, Markton's one and only market. It probably contained a get-well present for Pop. "How are you holding up?"

"Better now that we're home."

"You look tired." Lani studied Adele with a critical and unusually maternal eye.

"Actually, I'm feeling better than I did a while ago."

"Still getting queasy?"

"Sometimes," Adele answered reluctantly. This wasn't the first time Lani had inquired about her health, and she'd begun to regret mentioning her intermittent bouts of nausea. "If you want to visit Pop, you'll have to wait or come back. He's napping."

"I really came to see you." Lani set the sack on the table.

"Something the matter?" Fresh worries immediately sprang to Adele's mind. Was her mother's job at the feed store not working out? Did she want to return to the ranch? And get her old one back?

"No. Not with me, at least." Lani's expression was kind and filled with a concern Adele hadn't seen in years. "You've not been yourself lately."

"I have a lot going on at the moment," she said, a bit testily.

"I know you do. You're tired and irritable and—"

"Stress does that to a person."

"So does pregnancy."

The comment came so far from left field, Adele couldn't immediately absorb it. "I'm… not pregnant."

"Are you sure? You have the symptoms."

"Why would you… That's ridiculous!" She wasn't about to admit to her mother that she and Ty had been intimate, or discuss the type of protection they'd used.

"If you're not pregnant, then it could be something else. Better to know for sure." Lani opened the grocery sack and withdrew a box. "I bought this for you. I figured you wouldn't want to. Not in Markton. One thing I've learned since moving here is that folks *love* to gossip."

Adele stared at the home pregnancy test,

not sure what shocked her the most—her mother having the gall to butt into her personal life, or the possibility that she really was pregnant.

When was her last period?

She'd been too busy with Pop and his surgery to think about it. Now that she did, she realized she was late. By several weeks.

It couldn't be! She and Ty were careful.

But condoms weren't foolproof. And he'd said he'd been carrying that one in his wallet a long time.

Adele had to sit down before her knees buckled. With an unsteady hand, she pulled out a kitchen chair. Her mother was talking, but the words were only partially registering.

"This is one of those twin-pack early pregnancy tests. I didn't know if maybe you wanted to take one test this afternoon and then the second one tomorrow, just to be sure."

"Take the test now?"

"It's pretty simple." Through a fog, Adele watched her mother remove the kit from the package and unfold the instructions. "It's been a while since I've used one of these, but I doubt they've changed much in the last ten years."

Little by little, the enormity of the situation began to sink in. Adele could indeed be pregnant. Or not. Either way, she needed to find out.

"How does it work?" she asked in a weak voice, taking the testing kit from Lani.

While her mother read the instructions out loud, she rolled the wand between her fingers. Then she went to the hall bathroom and completed the test.

She waited the required time, sitting on the closed toilet-seat lid, an undefined ache lodged beneath her breast. Under different circumstances—if she and Ty were married, for instance—this would be a joyous occasion. Except they weren't married. They hadn't even discussed anything beyond dating.

Her mind swirled as question after question formed.

What about Pop and work and the ranch? She was only just beginning to grapple with the likelihood of having to take on additional tasks in the coming months. A child would triple her responsibilities. How would she cope?

Maybe she wouldn't have to. The results might be negative.

She gazed down at the testing wand in her hand, the plus sign clearly visible now. Even so, she squinted, doubting what her eyes saw.

Then it hit her. An emotion that could only be described as elation. It crashed over her in waves, bringing a huge smile to her face.

A baby! She was having a baby.

Adele stepped from the bathroom and into the kitchen, the testing wand extended in front of her.

Lani stood, her face expectant. An affection Adele hadn't felt for her mother in years filled her, and she impulsively opened her arms. Lani rushed to her, returning the hug *and* the affection.

"Well?" she asked when they separated.

Adele showed her the wand, and Lani, too, broke into a radiant smile.

"I'm going to be a grandmother."

Chapter 13

Adele stood in the middle of Pop's kitchen with her mother, dazed and a little in awe at the realization that she was pregnant.

Possibly pregnant, she amended. As the package instructions recommended, she should take the test again tomorrow morning just to be sure.

Except Adele *was* sure. The undefined ache she'd felt earlier had actually been her heart growing bigger with love for the tiny baby she carried. Soon her entire life would change, and in ways she could only imagine.

What about Ty's life? It would change, too.

Adele had been so preoccupied with herself, she'd failed to consider him.

How, she wondered, would he react? With happiness? Anger? They'd talked about their respective families many times, but not about starting one of their own. Certainly not this soon. Why would they? While their relationship had moved quickly, the fact was she and Ty had been dating only a couple of months, and half that time he'd been on the road.

She'd *have* to consider him, however, and soon.

But not yet. Not until she'd taken the second test and given herself a few days to reflect on her pregnancy and all the ramifications. There was also Pop and his recovery requiring her full and immediate attention.

Suddenly overwhelmed by everything she was facing, she sat back down at the table. Lani, beaming like a million-dollar lottery winner, joined her.

"How did you know?" Adele asked.

Her mom laughed. "I've been pregnant before. I recognized the symptoms."

That was a long time ago, Adele thought. Had being a mother made such an impression that Lani remembered even the smallest details twenty-eight years later?

"Did you have a lot of morning sickness?"

"With you? Heavens, no. I never felt better. With the…" Lani paused, guilt reflected in her eyes. The moment didn't last. Forcing a smile, she picked up right where she'd left off. "Some women are sick day and night."

The remark her mother had made earlier about home pregnancy tests not changing much in ten years came back to Adele.

"Were you pregnant more than once?"

Lani's eyes closed and her posture sagged. "Me and my big mouth."

"Mom?"

"I never wanted you to find out."

"What happened?"

"After you were born, I got pregnant again. But I lost the baby. A little boy."

"I'm so sorry. How terrible for you."

"It was hard. On your dad, too. Neither of us talked much about it, but soon after that he started drinking heavily."

"Why didn't you tell me?"

Lani patted Adele's hand, the first spontaneously caring gesture she'd made in years. If any barriers had remained between them, they vanished in that moment.

"It wasn't a burden I wanted you to bear."

"What happened ten years ago?"

Lani wiped her misty eyes and shook her head as if chiding herself for once again saying too much. "I got pregnant yet again, if you can believe it. But I guess it wasn't meant to be, because before I could even tell the baby's father, I miscarried." She let out a wistful sigh. "I had nothing but trouble after that. Female trouble. I finally got a hysterectomy this past March."

A hysterectomy? Was that the reason her mother had looked so thin and frail when she'd first arrived at Seven Cedars?

"But enough of that talk. You don't need to be hearing any of it. Not now." She patted Adele's cheek. "You're going to have a beautiful, healthy baby, and I'm going to be a grandmother. You should make an appointment with an obstetrician right away."

"I will." Maybe she could arrange that for next week, when she drove Pop to the medical center for his checkup and physical therapy.

"Not that it's any of my business, but when are you going to tell Ty?"

Adele didn't know how to answer her mother.

If she told him she was pregnant, he might quit rodeoing. No, he *would* quit. He'd probably propose, too, and move to Seven Cedars, believing marrying her to be the right and honorable thing to do.

She couldn't let him. Not that the idea of marrying Ty wasn't appealing...and there was the baby to consider. But what about the championship? He'd lost once before, when it was just within his grasp. Then there were his parents. They could really use the money he owed them. If he won, he could repay them every dime. For a man with Ty's pride, settling his debts was not just important, it was imperative.

Mentally counting backward, Adele determined that she was around six weeks pregnant, give or take. Plenty of time before she had to decide what to do. Before she began showing.

She suddenly remembered he was flying in Sunday evening. How could she see him, look at him, *be* with him, and not think of the baby? Maybe she should call him and postpone his trip, citing Pop as an excuse. Give herself a little more time to come to grips with...everything.

"I don't know when I'll tell him," Adele murmured contemplatively. "I want to see the doctor first. Make sure the baby's okay."

"Oh, honey bun." Lani's features fell. "I've

scared you with my stories, and I shouldn't have. Shame on me."

"I'm glad you told me." Adele welcomed the change in subject. "It explains a lot. I've been blaming you, and to a lesser degree, Dad, for things that weren't your fault. I think I have a lot of making up to do with both of you."

"That's sweet of you to say, but the truth is, I was a lousy mother. I hope you won't hold that against me, because I intend to be the best grandmother in the world."

"Good." Adele inhaled deeply. "I'm going to need a lot of help."

They reached across the table and shared another hug, only to be interrupted by a loud banging noise from down the hall.

"Pop!" Adele sprang from her chair.

Lani followed her to his bedroom. They were both aghast to find him sitting up in bed, his lap table on the floor and his walker leaning at a crooked angle.

"What are you doing?" Adele cried.

"Trying to get up. What the hell does it look like?" he barked, his face flushed a deep crimson.

"Are you in pain?" She glanced at the nightstand, where she'd left his medications, then at the clock. His next dose wasn't due for another two hours.

"Hell, yes, I'm in pain. I just had my hip replaced with some damn metal contraption."

"Oh, Pop," she soothed, wishing she could wave her hand and magically erase his suffering.

To her surprise, he let out a choked sob. "Why didn't you tell me you were having a baby?"

He must have heard her and Lani talking in the kitchen!

Before Adele could tell him she'd just found out herself, she was slammed with a wave of intense nausea, and barely reached the hall bathroom in time.

"Hey, Boudeau." A man Ty had handily beaten in steer wrestling that morning jogged toward him, tugging the brim of his ball cap down against the pouring rain. "What's the rush?" he hollered.

"Besides this weather?" Ty tossed his overnight bag into the backseat of Garth's pickup truck. It landed atop a plastic crate, rain gear, a laptop case and a well-worn duffel bag.

"A bunch of us are heading to the Chuck Box Bar and Grill," the man said upon reaching Ty. "You and Maitland want to come along?"

"Thanks, but we can't." He slammed the truck door shut, sidestepping a rapidly growing puddle. "I've got a plane to catch in two hours, and thirty miles to drive."

Garth had volunteered to drive him to the airport. Barring any traffic delays due to the rain, or longs lines at airport security, he had just enough time to make his flight.

"Guess I'll see you in Fort Benton."

"That you will."

Lifting the collar of his jacket, the man departed, his hunched form leaping over streams of running water.

Luckily for the participants, the weather had held for most of the rodeo. Saddle bronc riding, the last event of the day, had turned into a mud-flying free-for-all, and the closing ceremony was canceled. Ty hadn't minded. He'd grabbed his winnings and buckle— only one this weekend—and hightailed it to where he'd parked, meeting the friend who had agreed to drive his truck and trailer to her place in the next town over. Ty had known Nancy and her brother for years, and was confident Hamm couldn't have a better caretaker. When Ty returned from seeing Adele, Nancy would meet him at the airport and give him a lift to her place. From there, he would continue on to Fort Benton.

A lot of trouble and a lot of favors called in, but Ty felt it would be worth everything and more to see Adele.

He'd originally arranged for Nancy to drive him to the airport, but when Garth got wind of Ty's plans, he'd insisted on taking her place. A consolation prize, perhaps, for beating the pants off Ty earlier today.

And speaking of Garth…

Ty checked the time on his cell phone, cupping his hand to protect it from the rain. Where the heck was he? If they didn't head out soon, Ty might miss his plane.

He turned to see Garth running toward him, water exploding in great sheets from his boots as they hit the ground. Ty hated to think how soaked his friend's feet must be getting. Hopefully, he had an extra pair of shoes buried in that pile of stuff in his backseat.

"Sorry I'm late. I needed a pick-me-up for the road." Garth lifted his rain poncho and removed two large travel cups of coffee he'd been carrying. By some miracle, they'd survived the journey intact.

Ty took the one Garth held out to him.

"Thanks." He hoped the hot liquid would act like high-octane fuel, combating the sluggishness brought on by two days of intense competition and not enough sleep.

They climbed into the truck and began slowly traversing the muddy lake that had once been the parking area. Deep ruts hampered their progress. Ty had to force himself to keep from checking the time every few minutes. There was nothing he could do about the weather, so he might as well relax.

Yeah, right.

He tried distracting himself by guzzling coffee and listening, at least a little, to Garth ramble on about Reese and their upcoming wedding.

"We finally set a date. Valentine's Day. Reese insisted we wait until after Nationals. You're coming to the wedding, aren't you?"

"You still going to want me there when I take away your title?"

"After this weekend, I wouldn't bet on that."

Both men laughed. Ty wasn't worried. He might not have won every event today, but his scores were good enough to put him one step closer to qualifying for the National Finals Rodeo.

They were about a mile down the road when Ty's cell phone rang. His pulse jumped at seeing Adele's name flashing on the display. In a few hours, they'd be together. He dreaded thinking about the months stretching ahead of them until December. Instead of becoming easier, the separations were harder and harder. When he returned to Markton for Garth's wedding—and he would, win or lose—he planned on staying a full month with Adele. Maybe by then he could convince her to go with him to visit his parents.

"Hey, girl. How you doing?"

"Hanging in there."

Slouching in the seat, he readied himself for a long talk. While he couldn't pinpoint anything specific, she'd sounded odd the last few days. When he questioned her, she'd blamed her grandfather. Ty understood. Taking care of Pop couldn't be easy, though Adele swore he was doing remarkably well.

Ty promised himself she'd get as much rest as possible during his visit, even if it meant he had to play nursemaid to Pop. As long as he and Adele had their nights together...

"You have no idea how good it is to hear your voice," he said.

Beside him, Garth made a sound of disgust,

as if to imply Ty was nothing but a sucker for a pretty woman. The grin he wore, however, said Ty was in good company.

The two them were a pair, and Ty had to chuckle. Like Garth, he'd found the woman of his dreams. Ty also thought he might have found the place where he wanted to settle down for the rest of his life. Much as he loved Santa Fe, Wyoming had a lot more to offer. When he wasn't on the circuit, he could teach roping. Construct saddles in his spare time. Train with Garth. Woo Adele.

Life couldn't get any better. Except maybe with winning the title of World Champion.

"How'd you do today?" Adele asked.

"First in team roping. Second in steer wrestling." He shot Garth a dirty look. "Fourth in tie-down roping."

"Not bad."

"Fort Benton's going to be a whole 'nother story."

"You think," Garth muttered.

Ty ignored him, preferring to concentrate on Adele. "What's the latest on Pop?"

"Improving."

"Your mom?"

"Fine."

Her monosyllabic answers bothered him. "Is everything okay?"

"Great."

"What about Ritz?"

"Getting big."

Just when he was beginning to really worry, she asked, "Have you left for the airport yet?"

"On our way. Should be there in about forty-five minutes." She didn't immediately reply, and he thought they might have lost their connection. "You there?"

"Yeah." Another long pause followed. "Ty, I hate to ask this of you...."

"What's wrong?" Alerted by her tone, he sat bolt upright.

"Is there any chance you can postpone your trip?"

"Postpone? Why?"

Garth glanced over at him questioningly. Ty shrugged, not sure yet what was happening.

"I'm sorry." Adele sounded as if she was on the verge of crying.

"Sweetheart, what happened?"

"Nothing. It's just not a good time. Pop requires so much care—"

"I thought you said he was improving."

"Did I? Well, he is. I mean, the surgery site's healing. The, um, physical therapy isn't progressing at the speed the doctor wants."

"You told me yesterday he was almost ready for a cane."

"He is. He will be. Eventually. The therapists want me to take him in for an extra session this week."

"I'll go with you. Heck, I'll take him. You can stay home and nap. I know you're working your tail off." He wished she'd relinquish even a small amount of her grandfather's care to someone else rather than doing it all herself.

"It's not only Pop. We have…we have new calves arriving tomorrow, which I need to oversee. And the grain shipment's being delivered on Thursday."

"Can't the barn manager handle that?"

"He's, um, sick. The flu."

With sudden certainty, Ty knew Adele was lying. The question was why?

He immediately assumed the worst, and his stomach tightened into a knot. "You don't want to see me?"

"Of course I do!"

Ty sensed Garth's curious gaze on him,

but he couldn't be bothered with his friend right now.

"I'm just so overwhelmed." A tiny sob had crept into her voice. "I really do want to see you."

For the first time since she'd called, he felt she truly meant what she said. "I want that, too. Like crazy."

"Next week will be better," she added, suddenly more composed. "Or the week after. By then Pop should be getting around better, and won't be so demanding."

"Is he giving you that much of a hard time?"

"More than you know," she answered tiredly.

Perhaps Ty was reading too much into her request. It could be exactly as she claimed, and she wanted him to come out when her grandfather was more self-sufficient and her own energy not so depleted.

It occurred to him to fly out anyway, regardless of what she said. Every bone in his body longed to do just that.

"Please, Ty," she implored. "I need a little more time."

Desperate as he was to see her, he wouldn't make her life more difficult. "I'll reschedule my flight for next week."

"Or two weeks."

He'd be in Albuquerque then. And his family had talked about coming out to watch him compete. No problem. He'd find a way to make it work. "All right. Two weeks."

"Thank you."

"Hey, Stick called me the other day."

"He did?" She sounded alarmed.

"Said he was trying to get you to hire his cousin."

"Oh, yeah."

"Asked me if I—"

"Ty, I've got to go."

"Is it Pop?"

"Y-yes. He's calling me. Sorry. Bye."

Ty flipped his phone shut and stared out the window at the downpour.

"Everything okay?" Garth asked, taking his eyes momentarily off the road.

"I'm not sure." Ty removed his cowboy hat and flung it on the truck floor with more force than necessary. "Any way you can turn this vehicle around? We need to head back."

"Forget something?"

"Seems I'm not flying out today."

After a quick explanation, Ty called the airlines. Then he phoned Nancy. She expressed sympathy over his canceled trip, and readily agreed to meet him and Garth at the rodeo grounds.

"I appreciate all your help," he told Garth, then picked up his hat, brushed it off and returned it to his head.

"No problem."

After another mile, he said, "You know Adele pretty well, right?"

"Since we were kids."

"Tell me, how is she at handling stress?"

"You kidding? She's a rock. I remember when she and Pop started Cowboy College. Everything they had to go through to get it off the ground. And when her grandmother died, Adele was the one who held Pop together. He'd have drowned in his own grief without her."

Ty frowned.

"Why?"

"She's having a difficult time coping with Pop's hip-replacement surgery. I guess he's being irritable and demanding."

"When isn't he? She's used to that."

Yeah, she was.

"And she's got all kinds of help there," Garth continued. "Built-in food service, housekeeping and drivers if she needs them.

There's not an employee on the ranch who wouldn't pitch in if she asked them."

That was what Ty thought, too. "So why is she acting the way she is?"

Garth mulled the question over. "You really want my opinion?"

"I wouldn't ask if I didn't."

"There's something else going on," he said, confirming Ty's suspicions. "Something she's not telling you."

Pop hobbled into Adele's office without knocking, awkwardly closing the door behind him. During the three and a half weeks since his surgery, he'd graduated from the walker to a cane, and was getting around quite well.

Enough that he'd decided two days ago he was ready to resume his previous responsibilities. Adele would have none of it, convinced he'd trip on something and injure his brand-new hip. Stick had been assigned to drive Pop wherever he wanted to go in the golf cart, and to keep an eye on him. Fortunately for Adele's nerves, Pop tired easily and had yet to do more than chat with the barn manager, watch a few classes and check out the new grain shipment.

He also made trips to her office to inquire about the running of the ranch.

She bore those visits as patiently as possible.

Except when he asked about the baby. Other than to respond that she was feeling well despite continued morning sickness, she clammed up. Pop gave new meaning to the word *relentless* and was constantly pushing her to do what he thought was right, namely tell Ty about the baby and, as Pop put it, make an honest woman out of her.

She refused to argue, as determined as her grandfather to handle the situation her own way. Which, at the moment, was to do and say nothing.

"Hey, Pop. What brings you here?" She smiled brightly, already knowing the answer and bracing herself for a string of questions about reservations, food orders and class schedules.

"What time is Ty arriving?" He bent and grabbed her visitor's chair, pulling it away from the wall.

Adele automatically leaped up to help him.

"Sit your fanny down," he grumped. "I can manage. Don't need you hovering every second of the day." And he did manage. Just fine.

Was it true? Did she hover?

Probably.

She sat poised on the edge of her seat until Pop leaned his cane against her file cabinet, exhaling lustily as he did.

"We had two new reservations," she said, facing her computer and moving her mouse. "At this rate—"

"When is Ty getting in?" he repeated.

"After lunch sometime," Adele answered, hoping her tone gave no indication how nervous she was about his visit.

"Where's he staying?"

"Room nine's vacant."

"It's a little small for him."

"Better than his horse trailer."

At the mention of Ty's trailer, Adele was inundated with memories of when they'd made love in his tiny living quarters. Consulting the calendar after her trip to the obstetrician's office, she felt certain that was the night she'd gotten pregnant.

"If you need to rent the room out, he can bunk in my house."

"I don't need to rent it out."

She didn't mention that Ty would probably stay with her.

"You going to tell him about the baby?"

Pop had asked the question no less than two dozen times.

Her answer was always the same. "Eventually."

"Eventually over the next two days or eventually sometime before the kid's born?"

"I'll tell him when the moment's right."

He grumbled an expletive under his breath. "You can't hide this forever."

"No. But I can for a while."

"Dellie," Pop warned.

She opened her mouth to object, then promptly closed it at the sight of his watery eyes. Struck by a rush of tender emotions, she got up and went to him, stooping over to give him a loving hug.

"I can't believe I'm going to be a great-grandfather," he mumbled. "Your grandmother would be overjoyed. God, I wish she was here."

"Me, too." Adele swallowed a sob.

"I know you think I'm being a crotchety old busybody."

"Did I say that?"

"I only want what's best for you and the baby. And that's a father. A father *and* a husband."

Adele returned to her desk chair. "You need to let me and Ty work this out between us."

"Don't know why you're taking so long," Pop complained, back to his former grumpy self.

She didn't mind. He put on a gruff front, but deep down he was a sentimental slob.

"I need time, Pop. This is a big deal. Life altering. For both of us."

"Are you afraid he's going to leave you high and dry?"

"No. Just the opposite, in fact."

"As it should be. He has a responsibility." Her grandfather's voice rose.

Adele glanced worriedly at the office door, then shushed him. "But not one he asked for or planned on so soon in our relationship," she said in a subdued voice.

"He's a good man, Dellie. He'll take care of you and the baby."

"I know. But an unplanned pregnancy isn't an automatic reason to rush into marriage. There are other things to consider. Other people."

"Just because your folks were lousy parents, don't assume you and Ty will be, too."

Her grandfather's words sliced into her,

opening wounds she thought were finally closed.

"That's not it."

"Are you sure?"

"Yes," she replied. Only she wasn't. Not entirely.

Already she loved the baby with every breath she drew, and wanted more than anything for him or her to have a better childhood than she'd had. Two parents, Adele knew, was no guarantee for happiness.

Her cell phone abruptly rang. "It's Ty," she told her grandfather, after checking the screen, and answered with a forced but chipper, "Hello."

"I'm pulling in the drive."

"Already!"

"I couldn't wait to see you."

His enthusiasm was catching. "I can't wait to see you, either."

"Where are you?"

"My office."

"Meet me out front in two minutes."

Adele was instantly on her feet. "You coming?" she asked Pop, after disconnecting.

"Naw. You go on. I'll meet up with him later."

"Promise me you won't say anything about the baby until I've talked to him."

Pop grumbled his assent.

She was out the door and halfway across the lobby when she remembered she hadn't made sure he could rise from the chair without assistance. Starting back, she halted when he appeared in her office doorway.

"Get going." He shooed her away. "I'm fine."

Standing on the front porch, she watched Ty's truck approach, toy-size at first, then growing larger as it neared.

He had come home to Seven Cedars. And *her*.

All at once, happiness bubbled up inside her, vanquishing her earlier doubts and insecurities. Whatever obstacles they faced, and there were a lot of them, they'd find a solution. Together. The sight of his grinning face, full of gladness and affection, further convinced her that nothing was impossible.

She ran down the steps and into his arms the instant he climbed out of his truck.

"I have some great news!"

"So do I," he said, giving her a smacking kiss on the lips.

She laughed, giddy with delight. "You go first."

"Big Sky Trailers has offered me a sponsorship contract with a bonus if I win at Nationals."

"They did?"

"It's only a one-year contract to start, but they're talking magazine ads and even cable TV spots if all goes well."

"That's…wonderful."

"I'll have to go to Texas for the month of January. That's where their headquarters is located."

Adele's heart went from beating wildly to skipping painfully. So much for springing her announcement on him.

"Can you believe it?" He lifted her off her feet, swung her in a circle and gave her another kiss. "Hey, I missed breakfast this morning and I'm starving. Any chance the dining hall's still open? We can talk about why you've been avoiding me over lunch."

Chapter 14

Pop had joined Adele and Ty for lunch. With his mouth set in a grim line, he sat listening to Ty expound on the details of the Big Sky Trailers sponsorship contract, which were exciting to say the least.

Exciting for Ty.

"If I win at Nationals, they want to feature me and Hamm in their advertising campaign." He seemed to have forgotten all about her news. Perhaps that was for the best. "Even more incentive for me to win," he said with single-minded determination.

Ty was well on the way to getting everything he wanted. Not at all like when he'd first come to Cowboy College...what? Nearly three months ago.

Adele was partially responsible for the transformation. Little had she known at the time that helping him fix his problems with Hamm and launch a career comeback would return to hurt her.

Little had she known she'd fall in love with him.

She pressed a hand to her breast, trying to soothe the ragged pain beneath it. Given the chance to do it all over again, she'd change nothing. Not loving him and certainly not having his baby.

"Of course, I'll be here for Garth and Reese's wedding," he continued, finishing the last of his steak sandwich.

Pop hadn't ordered any food, and Adele only picked at her shrimp salad. Ty didn't appear to notice their lack of appetites.

"That's good," she said, mentally calculating which stage she'd be in her pregnancy come Valentine's Day. No hiding it then. Even if she tried, someone was bound to say something.

"Why don't you come with me to Texas?" He reached under the table and rested a hand on her knee, his eyes alight with boyish charm. "You can visit your dad. Big Sky's headquarters is only a couple hours from where he lives."

When Adele didn't immediately respond, Pop made a disgruntled sound, which Ty misinterpreted.

"Sorry, Pop. I should've talked to you first about stealing her away."

"Not my decision," he muttered crustily.

It was on the tip of Adele's tongue to explain her grandfather's dour mood, only she couldn't think of anything to say without mentioning the baby. Instead, she asked Ty, "Is this what you want? The sponsorship contract?"

He gave her a surprised look. "It's a great opportunity. And not just because of the money."

She nodded. No argument there. "I thought you wanted to build saddles."

"Charlie's shop will be there when I'm ready."

Adele couldn't help but wonder if he planned to include her in his long-term goals. He'd made no mention of the future other than her accompanying him to Texas in January.

Wasn't she just as guilty of making plans without him?

Not the same, she told herself. She *was* thinking of him.

Ty would quit competing and give up a lucrative sponsorship the moment he learned about the baby. It wasn't fair, not when he'd worked so hard and so long to achieve his dream. Neither was it fair to make his parents wait additional months, perhaps years, for the money he owed them. Especially when they could really use it and had already been exceedingly patient.

She could see why the Big Sky's marketing people had approached Ty. Not only was his meteoric return to roping catching the attention of fans, he was a great spokesperson, possessing good looks, talent and a natural charm. Not to mention a gorgeous and athletic horse. Some ropers competed their whole lives and had little to show for it. Ty could, if all went well, build an impressive career from this one sponsorship offer.

She wouldn't be the one to take it from him.

"We don't have to decide anything right this second," she said cheerfully, attempting to smooth out the awkward pause.

Her smile must have appeared as fake as it

felt, for Ty stopped eating, set his fork down and turned to her.

"I haven't signed the contract yet. I can always change my mind."

"It's a great offer. You'd be a fool not to take it."

Pop's closed hand came down a little too hard on the table.

Ty's gaze darted to him, then back to Adele. "Yes, but I don't want to be away from you."

"We'll talk more tonight," she told him, her fake smile still firmly in place.

Pop grumbled angrily and, leaning heavily on his cane, rose from the table. Without a word, he limped away.

"I guess I upset him."

"It's not you." Adele also stood, and patted Ty's shoulder. "I'll be right back."

He stopped her by snaring her wrist. "Are we okay? Are *you* okay?"

She didn't answer him. "Give me a few minutes alone with Pop, will you?"

His eyes followed her as she hurried out of the dining hall. She could only guess what he was thinking.

Spying Pop outside, she called to him. "Wait."

He halted, but one glance at his fierce expression had her wishing she'd let him go on ahead without her.

"You need to tell him about the baby," he barked when she was within earshot.

"Not so loud." She tugged on his arm imploringly. "You know what will happen if I do. He'll stay here and give up the Big Sky sponsorship contract. Quit team roping with Garth. Probably propose to me."

"As he should!"

"What makes you think I want to marry him?"

Pop gaped at her. "Why the hell not?"

Adele grimaced and moved in front of him, as if that would stop his voice from carrying to the guests nearby. "He already lost one championship and one career opportunity. I don't want to be the reason he loses a second one. I certainly don't want to be the reason his mother loses her real estate business."

"We could lend him the—"

"Do you think for one second Ty would take money from us?"

"He might. If you two were married."

"No, he won't. He has too much pride. Just like he'll quit competing if I tell him about the baby. He'd want any child of his to have two parents at home. Like he did. Like I didn't."

Pop grumbled.

"I can't risk Ty coming to resent me for taking everything away from him. And he will, even if he doesn't mean to. Worse, he might come to resent our child."

"Dellie."

She hugged her grandfather, hating the frailty in his frame, which hadn't been there before. "The best day of my life was when I came here to live permanently." The best day until she'd learned she was pregnant. "I want my child to grow up with everything you and Grandma gave me. A good home, security, wide-open spaces and the best horses in the state to ride." She wiped her damp cheeks.

"I can't take the place of a father."

"You did for me."

"I still think you should tell Ty." Though Pop continued insisting, much of the fight had gone out of him.

"I will someday, but not right now."

He ruffled her hair as he had when she was young. "I love you, Dellie."

"I love you, too, Grandpa."

He chuckled, though it was filled with sadness. "You haven't called me Grandpa since you were fourteen."

"Maybe I should start again."

"Whatever excuse you're going to give Ty, you'd better think fast." Pop tilted his head toward the lobby door. "Because here he comes."

Adele's pulse spiked at the sight of Ty striding in her direction, looking every bit like a man who wouldn't settle until he knew what the heck was going on.

Adele didn't have a destination in mind when she and Ty started walking. After a few minutes, she noticed their feet were taking them to the corral where Stick had placed Hamm while they had lunch with Pop. Probably because the corral was away from the ranch hands and guests, and gave them a modicum of privacy.

"What's wrong?" Ty demanded when they neared the fence. Given how poorly he was concealing his frustration, she was impressed he'd waited. "And this time, Adele, I want an answer. No more sidestepping."

Having little experience in breaking up with men, she decided quick and clean was the best approach.

Easier on you, too, a small voice inside her whispered.

True. But why prolong the agony?

Sticking to her hastily concocted plan, she

blurted, "I've recently realized I'm not cut out for a long-distance relationship."

Ty visibly jerked and his eyes widened, but when he spoke, his words were measured, as if he was weighing each one. "It's only been a couple of months."

Good point. And if not for the baby, she'd be willing to give their arrangement a considerably longer trial period.

"I don't need any more time. This isn't working out for me."

"I'd have come two weeks ago. You're the one who told me not to."

"Pop just had surgery."

"And I respected your wishes. Now, all of a sudden, you tell me it's not working out, and act as if it's my fault, when you're the one pushing me away."

He was absolutely right.

Nonetheless, Adele continued, afraid her courage would desert her. "You have every right to be angry at me."

"I'm not angry, I'm confused."

She could see it clouding his eyes, along with the hurt she was inflicting.

Damn. She'd been in such a hurry, she hadn't considered he might put up a fight. She was, however, committed to finish what she'd begun. They would both come away from this bruised and possibly a little embittered, but everyone would be better off in the long run.

"The reason my parents' marriage fell apart was because Dad only stayed home a few months of the year."

"Is that what you want?" Ty asked. "For us to get married?"

It was her turn to jerk. "No!"

"Why not?"

She drew a shallow breath. Anything deeper was impossible, not with the huge knot of pain pressing against her ribs. "Seven Cedars is my home, and Cowboy College is my business. I'm not leaving either of them. Asking you to give up your home and your dream isn't right, either."

"I don't get it." He rubbed the back of his neck, his jaw working furiously. "Why can't we continue the way we are?"

"Because my heart shatters every time you leave and every time you hang up the phone after calling me." That much, at least, was completely true.

"And you think the answer is to break up with me?"

Adele involuntarily crossed her arms over her middle. "Yes."

"Have you met somebody else?"

"Of course not!"

He shook his head, his brows forming a deep V. "This makes no sense."

Hamm must have sensed the seriousness of their mood. Rather than trot in circles as usual, he stood solemnly in the center of the corral, head lowered, tail swishing, his breath stirring up small dust clouds.

"I'm sorry," Adele murmured.

"Just like that? You break up with me out of the blue, tell me you're sorry, and I'm supposed to be okay with it?" Ty might not have been angry before, but he definitely was now.

"Please try and see this from my side."

"How much does this have to do with the sponsorship offer from Big Sky?"

He'd finally put two and two together.

"Some," she admitted.

"Because I'll be gone the month of January?"

"Nationals isn't until late December. Add January, when you'll be in Texas, and you're asking me to wait half a year."

"We'd see each other every few weeks."

"For a day or two."

"I have a break over the holidays."

"What about next year?"

"Who says I'll compete next year?"

"You know you will. You told me you wanted to compete until you physically couldn't anymore."

"I…" He hesitated and shifted awkwardly.

Was this the moment she'd been hoping for? When he'd tell her he loved her? She chewed her bottom lip, waiting…and waiting.

"I…care about you. A lot. I'm not ready for this to end."

If he only knew how much she wasn't ready for this to end, either.

She could always tell him she'd had a change of heart. They would kiss, make up and pretend this morning had never happened.

Except what would that accomplish other than delaying the inevitable? Unless she was prepared to tell him about the baby, be the reason he quit competing, forfeited the championship, postponed paying back his parents, she had to let him go. Now.

"I'm being selfish, I know that," she said. "The idea of ending up like my mother… I won't let that happen to me."

"I'm not your father."

"No, but you'll be gone as much as he was."

"I just don't understand why you can't come with me sometimes. I'm not asking you to leave the ranch for weeks on end."

"You saw Pop. He can't get through a day without taking a nap. How's he going to run this place by himself, even for a weekend? We're also smack-dab in the middle of our busy season."

"Those are excuses." He narrowed his eyes, as if trying to read more into what she said. "If you really wanted to take a few vacation days, you could."

"They're valid excuses." Adele refused to wilt under his penetrating stare. "I can't turn my back on my family and my business. A lot of people depend on me."

"So do I."

He depended on her? For what? Help with his horse? A place to crash between competitions? Disappointment sliced through her.

"I wish things were different."

"You're not giving me a choice." His anger had returned, lending his voice a steely edge.

"And what choice would that be? Have me wait for you for what could be years? Give up my life here, my home and my business?

Leave my ailing grandfather? That's asking a lot."

Her words were harsh, as she'd intended. In response, his expression closed, like a door slamming shut.

She clenched her hands into fists and held them at her sides. It was the only way to prevent herself from going to him.

"Can we sleep on it? Talk again in the morning?"

His request was utterly reasonable. Except Adele knew if their breakup wasn't a swift one, she ran the risk of reconsidering and relenting. Or allowing Pop to sway her, as he would surely try to do if Ty stayed on the ranch. Even overnight.

"It won't make any difference."

She swore he flinched.

In that moment, Adele hated herself.

"If you ever—"

"I have to go."

Turning on her heel, she walked the entire distance to her apartment, without once stopping or looking back. Thankfully, Ty didn't follow her, saving her from having to test her willpower.

Oh, God, what must he think of her?

How could she have been so cruel?

In the solitude of her bedroom, she cried until a bout of nausea sent her running to the bathroom. A while later, Pop called to check on her and to let her know Ty had loaded Hamm and pulled out about thirty minutes earlier, telling no one where he was going.

Adele suspected he needed a friend about now and might head over to see Garth.

"Are you sure you didn't make a mistake, Dellie?" Pop asked.

She might have been able to lie to Ty, but her grandfather was a different story. "No, I'm not sure at all."

"When he finds out, and he will eventually, he's going to be mad."

She could deal with that. What she couldn't deal with was Ty hating her. And he very well could after what she'd done to him.

Chapter 15

"What's with you, bro? You suck today."

Ty's little sister, Dana, couldn't be more right. In the three weeks since Adele had given him his walking papers, he could hardly put his boots on the correct feet, much less rope. He wasn't just back to where he'd been after Nationals last year, he was worse. Worse than worse. He couldn't rope a calf if it climbed up in the saddle with him. Even Hamm snorted in disgust whenever Ty approached.

Dana circled the big gelding, studying him intently. "I don't see a thing wrong with him," she said, shaking her head contemplatively. "He's in great shape."

"I was afraid of that."

Dana had met up with Ty the evening before. He was in St. George for the Lions Dixie Roundup Rodeo. She'd traveled to a town twenty miles over the hill for a job interview with a prestigious equine hospital. Though he knew her side trip to St. George was a thinly disguised attempt to check up on him at the request of their parents, he was still glad to see her. Last night, over a couple of beers, she'd offered to examine Hamm, on the slim chance Ty's recent string of losses was due to an injury or illness.

As he'd expected, he had no one to blame but himself.

"What are you going to do?" Dana asked.

"About what?"

She ticked off the items on her fingers. "Competing tomorrow. Big Sky's offer. Adele."

"Nothing."

"Not a good answer."

"Keep trudging along."

She made a face. "Excuse my language, but you need to get your shit together."

He did. His standings were slipping. Fast. At this rate, he wouldn't qualify for Nationals. Big Sky's people had started getting a little antsy. If Ty didn't win or place in the top three soon, they might pull out of their contract, citing the clause that gave them the right to do so if he didn't perform at a certain level.

So much for paying his parents back in one lump sum.

His folks would cut him some slack. Continue being patient.

Ty, however, was fast losing all patience with himself. This wasn't how it was supposed to be.

"Have you talked to Adele since she kicked you to the curb?"

Ty winced. "Do you have to be so blunt?"

"Yes. Everyone's been walking on eggshells around you, afraid of saying the wrong thing because you might have a meltdown or cry or something. I say you need a good shaking up."

They were in the barn at the rodeo fairgrounds, standing in Hamm's stall. Leaving it, they latched the door behind them and headed down the aisle. Ty had competed yesterday in both team and tie-down roping, doing badly in the former, his lasso missing the calf by a good foot. Garth didn't say much afterward, taking the disqualification in stride. Ty half wished his partner would blow up at him. Maybe then he wouldn't feel so guilty.

Amazingly, he hadn't done quite so terribly in tie-down roping, currently holding sixth place. A position that landed him in the final round later today.

Big Sky Trailers, however, wasn't interested in a spokesman who came in sixth.

"The answer is no, I haven't spoken to Adele, and I'm not going to."

"Why not?" Dana pressed. "You're nuts about her."

"I won't beg."

He would, actually, if he thought it would do any good. Hell, he'd get down on his knees. But Adele's cold tone during their last meeting still haunted him, and he doubted she'd softened her stance since then.

"Who said anything about begging?" Dana sent him a conspiratorial smile. "I had sweet-talking in mind. And flowers."

Wildflowers. That's what he had given Adele before, and she'd liked them very much.

Ty pushed the memory away to a dark corner in his mind.

While Dana continued to yap about the pros and cons of various tokens of affection, they cut behind the main arena, bypassing the food and vendor booths and hordes of people milling about. By nine o'clock tonight, the rodeo would be over and the grounds resembling a ghost town.

Much the way Ty's insides felt.

He'd replayed his last conversation with Adele repeatedly in his head, unable to shake the feeling she hadn't been entirely honest with him. Try as he might, he could detect nothing specific in her words or actions, except one. When he'd said he depended on her, she had instantly withdrawn, emotionally and physically.

What a fool he'd been. Given a second chance, he would have hauled her into his arms, told her he loved her and kidnapped her to his trailer so they could relive their first night together.

Because he did love her. Ty realized that now. Much too late, unfortunately.

"Markton's a four-hour drive from here," Dana was saying. "You could head over tonight after the rodeo."

"I can't."

"I'll come with you," she added, as if she hadn't heard him.

His temper flared. "Butt out, sis."

They stopped and faced each other, Dana

with her hands on her hips, Ty with his teeth grinding together.

"Well, you need to do something. Cowboy College fixed you before. Maybe it can again."

Cowboy College? Or Adele?

He'd gone to Seven Cedars looking for that missing magical element that would turn Hamm and his good partnership to an unstoppable one. And he'd found it.

Not in the minor discoveries he'd made, such as how Hamm moved or which eye he took aim with. Ty had found it with Adele. Her belief in him and his desire to make her proud of him were what had inspired him to push himself harder than he ever had before.

"You're right," he told his sister, his anger dissolving. Not that he ever stayed angry at Dana long. "Cowboy College did fix me."

She grinned. "So, what are we waiting for? Let's go."

"If I do, I'd have to be willing to give up rodeoing, Nationals and the Big Sky sponsorship contract. For good. Adele doesn't want a man who's on the road all the time. That's why she kicked me to the curb in the first place."

Dana's expression turned serious. "Are you willing to do that?"

It was, he realized, the million-dollar question.

Adele drove straight from Pop's house to the main lodge and parked in front, leaving her truck sitting at a crooked angle. She'd been looking for her grandfather all over the ranch for the better part of an hour, with no luck. He hadn't shown up for class after breakfast, and according to everyone she asked, no one had seen hide nor hair of him all morning. Her mild concern over his abrupt disappearance was quickly blossoming into outright worry.

Where could he be?

Climbing the steps to the main lodge, she called his cell phone for the tenth time, angrily pressing the disconnect button when it went straight to his voice mail.

Did his battery die, or had he shut off his phone?

Not for the first time she wondered how much his disappearance had to do with their argument last night. Ever since Ty left Pop had been nagging her to tell him about the baby. Try as she might, she couldn't blame her grandfather. He was old-fashioned and set in his ways, and believed a man should be responsible for his children.

As Ty did.

Her throat ached at the thought of him. Not an hour passed that she didn't miss him and second-guess her decision to send him packing. It was crazy how completely he'd become a part of her life in just a few months.

Then again, with the baby she was carrying, he'd be a part of her life always. Even if he didn't know it.

Pushing thoughts of Ty to the back of her mind as she crossed the lobby, she concentrated on Pop. Wherever he was, he must have his truck. It wasn't in his garage or in his usual parking space at the barn.

After peeking in her office—a long shot, but she tried anyway—she went down the hall to the kitchen. If she didn't find him there, she was going into town and would scour it end to end. That failing, she was calling the sheriff. They probably wouldn't do anything, not until Pop had been missing twenty-four hours. Hopefully, they would put the word out to look for him and his vehicle. Especially when she explained about his bad arthritis and recent hip-replacement surgery.

All at once, she had a brainstorm. The Maitlands would help her search for Pop. She pulled out her cell phone to call Garth, only to pause. They were at the rodeo in St. George. Garth had mentioned the other day he and his family were all going.

Ty was there, too.

Returning her cell phone to her pocket, she pushed open the door to the kitchen and entered. The staff was busy preparing for lunch, and she didn't want to get in the way.

"Sorry to bother you," she called out. Heads turned in response. "Has anyone seen Pop?"

"Not since breakfast." Confirming nods accompanied the dishwasher's reply.

"Okay." Adele's spirits plummeted even as her worry escalated to new heights. "If anyone does see or hear from him, tell him to call me right away."

As she was leaving, she ran into Cook coming out of the walk-in freezer.

"What are you doing here, girl?" With her generous girth and perpetually red complexion, Cook resembled an overgrown cherub.

"Trying to find Pop."

"Well, he's not here." The woman chuckled.

"I know."

"He went to St. George. Left about a half hour ago."

"What?" Adele's jaw quite literally dropped. "You're kidding."

Cook looked perplexed, then alarmed. "Didn't he tell you?"

"No." Adele was torn between relief and irritation. Relief won out.

"He asked me to pack him a lunch. Said he'd be home by dinnertime."

"What was he thinking? He can't drive that far. Not at his age and with his hip."

"I'm sorry, Adele. I had no idea he didn't tell you."

This wasn't Cook's fault. Adele tried to remain calm, knowing she'd have more luck stopping a moving freight train than Pop when he set his mind on something.

And Adele was fairly certain she knew what that something was.

He had gone to track down Ty and tell him about the baby.

Dammit. He had no right.

"I'm going after him," she told Cook, calculating how much of a head start her grandfather had on her. Luckily, he always drove five to ten miles under the speed limit. "I'll let you know when I find him."

Once in her truck, Adele made a series of phone calls. First to the barn manager, instructing him to have Stick cover the day's classes. Next, she called Garth and, getting his voice mail, left a message for him to keep an eye out for Pop at the rodeo. Lastly, she contacted the sheriff's office, just in case Pop had an accident or his truck broke down on the highway.

She considered calling Ty, then chickened out. He'd want to know why Pop was coming to see him, and Adele wasn't ready to explain.

In town, she stopped at the gas station to fill up. Just as she was returning the nozzle to the pump, her mother pulled up in her pint-size economy car and rolled down the window.

"Hey, Dellie. I was just on my way to see you. I know it's probably a little early for this, but I brought some nursery—"

"I can't talk now. Pop took off without telling me. He's on his way to St. George to find Ty. I'm going after him."

Lani didn't hesitate. "I'll come with you."

Until very recently, Adele would have refused to let her mother accompany her anywhere.

Not today.

"Park your car over there, and let's go."

* * *

Ty and Dana would have made better time getting Hamm to the warm-up arena if not for being waylaid by Mike and Sandy.

"What are you guys doing here?" Ty greeted his friends and former fellow students warmly.

"Mike surprised me with tickets," Sandy gushed.

Ty introduced Dana, and the four of them chatted amiably. Well, Dana did most of the chatting. Ty's mind was occupied elsewhere.

Funny how knowing what to do gave a man a sense of peace. As soon as he finished his event this afternoon, he'd load up and hit the road again.

Garth meandered over while they were talking, leading his own horse.

"You on your way to warm up?" he asked Ty, after saying hello to Mike, Sandy and Dana.

Ty started to answer, then was distracted by the sight of Pop emerging from the crowd and coming toward him. Ty's first thought was that Pop's limp had significantly lessened. The hip-replacement surgery was obviously a success.

"Hey, Pop." He smiled, ridiculously pleased

to see the older man. "What are you doing here?"

At his greeting, everyone in their group turned, matching smiles on their faces.

Ignoring them, Pop came straight at Ty, his wizened features fixed in a purposeful scowl, his stride deliberate. "I need to have a word with you, young man."

A word? Young man?

"Sure." Ty handed Hamm's reins to Dana and stepped forward. "Is something the matter?"

"This is for taking advantage of my little girl."

Before Ty could respond, Pop's fist connected with his jaw in a lightning fast right hook worthy of a man one-third his age.

Ty's head snapped to the side. Pain radiated through his entire face, neck and shoulders, and he stumbled backward from the force of the blow.

Sandy let out a little scream.

Ty shook his head, dazed and more than a little confused. It didn't occur to him to retaliate.

"And this is for leaving her in a fix."

Pop's left fist plowed into Ty's stomach, knocking the wind clean out of him and sending him sprawling to the ground, flat on his rear.

"Stop him," Dana cried.

"Hey, that's enough."

Ty heard Garth and his sister over the dense ringing in his ears, and had a vague impression of Garth scuffling with Pop and pulling him away. Thank God. Pop might be seventy-seven and suffering from debilitating arthritis, but he still packed a mean punch.

"What do you mean, I left her in a fix?" he sputtered, his knees bent and his throbbing head cradled in his hands. Fortunately, the ringing in his ears had started to subside.

"Dellie's pregnant."

"She is?" Squinting, he looked up at Pop, an action that sent fresh waves of pain pulsing through him.

"You're going to be a father."

"I am?" The blows he'd taken must have dulled his thinking, for nothing made sense.

"You all right?"

Mike's face appeared, and Ty had the impression of hands tenderly and expertly probing him all over for injuries. He was also aware of a growing audience.

"I don't know," he slurred, trying not to move his sore mouth.

"Sandy." Mike pulled a handkerchief from his back pocket. "Put some ice from your drink in this." She did and Mike pressed the ice pack to Ty's jaw, while Dana hovered nearby.

Garth knelt down beside Ty, his face splitting in a wide grin. "Congratulations, pal."

"She never said anything." Ty looked around for Pop. "I swear, if she had, I wouldn't have left her."

Suddenly, Garth, Dana, Mike and Sandy all stood and stepped away. Ty's vision had cleared enough for him to see Adele emerging from the crowd and running toward him, her mother and a security guard not far behind.

"What happened? Ty, are you okay?"

Adele took Garth's place, kneeling beside Ty. Mike went to talk to the security guard.

"Did you fall?" she asked, her touch more tender and more welcome than Mike's.

"Your grandfather slugged me. Twice."

"Pop!" Adele turned and sent her grandfather an infuriated glare. "I apologize for him," she said, returning her attention to Ty.

"How come you didn't tell me you're pregnant?"

"I—I…because I was afraid you'd quit rodeoing."

"Hell, yes, I will."

"You can't."

"I'm not leaving my—"

"You will not lose the championship again. You hear me? Too much is riding on it."

The side of his mouth that didn't ache pulled up in a smile. "Kind of bossy, aren't you?"

"I was wrong, Ty." She lowered her gaze. "I should have told you about the baby."

"Yes, you should have."

"It's just that you've worked so hard to get to this point, and you deserve to win."

"You deserve to have the father of your baby there with you when you need him." The fog around him had lifted. In fact, his head was clearer than it had been in weeks.

"What are you—"

"Shut up." Cupping her face in his hands, he drew her to him for a kiss that would have lasted longer if his mouth didn't hurt so much. "Help me up," he demanded when they broke apart.

"Are you sure you should? You could have broken something."

He beckoned to Garth to give him a boost. "I'm not going to propose to you sitting on my ass in the dirt."

"Propose!" Adele gasped. "We need to talk first."

"Plenty of time for that later." Pop sidled over to them.

"This is what you wanted." Adele stared at him accusingly.

"Damn straight," he said with undisguised satisfaction.

Sandy didn't hide her tears as she squeezed Mike's arm. "Isn't this romantic?"

Ty wasn't sure how getting the tar beaten out of him was romantic.

"Wait until Mom and Dad hear!" Dana exclaimed with glee, and whipped out her cell phone, taking pictures to commemorate the moment.

Adele rose along with Ty as Garth pulled him to his feet. He wobbled only for as long as it took him to put an arm around her and nestle her against him.

"I know there's a lot we need to figure out." Everything that had happened during his last visit to Seven Cedars suddenly made sense. And now that he understood her concerns, he would do everything in his power to lay them to rest. "We'll do it one day, one problem at a time."

"I don't want you marrying me because you feel obligated."

"I'm not. I love you, Adele. And I should have told you that weeks ago." He could see a trace of uncertainty in her expression. "Would it help you to know I was planning on driving to Seven Cedars tonight after the rodeo?"

"You were?"

"And when I got there, I was going to demand you give us a second chance."

"Oh, Ty. I love you, too."

"I'm glad you said that." He tugged her closer, threading his fingers in her hair. "So, how 'bout a September wedding?"

"Not so fast, cowboy." She leaned back, appraising him critically. "There's a little matter of the World tie-down roping and team roping championships."

"I thought we agreed—"

"We did no such thing. You're going to finish out the season. The baby will wait until then."

"What if I can't?" He felt his grin expand.

"You can come home every couple of weeks. And I'll fly out to see you. Once. Maybe twice." She was grinning, too. "If you win the championship, and only if you win, then I'll consider marrying you."

Her challenge was like the one she'd issued him at the Cowboy College jackpot. Then, it had been a dinner date at stake. Today, it was the rest of their lives.

"You think I can't?"

"I know you can't unless you qualify," she answered smugly.

Ty accepted his fallen hat from Garth, slapped it against his leg to knock off the dust and put in back on his head. "Seems I have an event to win."

"You sure you're up to it?" Mike asked with doctorly concern.

"I am." Ty only had eyes for Adele. "And when I do win, then we'll talk about *my* list of requirements."

She raised her brows in surprise. "Such as?"

"If I'm going to retire after Nationals, we make some changes at Cowboy College. I want to expand the program to include professional ropers. With three experts in residence, we can attract an entirely new clientele."

"And one on the way," Lani added. "With genes like theirs, how could the kid not be a roper?"

"I like it." Pop smiled approvingly and draped an arm around Lani.

"Me, too." Adele stood on tiptoes to give Ty's cheek a tender kiss.

"Hate to break up the party, buddy," Garth said, "but we'd better get a move on." He swung up into the saddle.

"No taking it easy on me just because I'm injured and newly engaged," Ty warned his friend.

"I wouldn't dream of it."

Much as Ty hated to, he left Adele to join Garth in the warm-up arena.

An hour later, the announcer's voice blared from the speakers, proclaiming Ty the tie-down roping winner. Amid the applause and cheers that followed, he shouted the news that Ty had set an arena record with his last run.

Ty hardly heard the man. He was too busy kissing his wife-to-be and the mother of his child, and planning their future, one that included the realization of all their dreams, a display cabinet full of gold belt buckles and a three-generation legacy to pass on to their children.

* * * * *

Get 4 FREE REWARDS!

We'll send you 2 FREE Books <u>plus</u> 2 FREE Mystery Gifts.

Love Inspired books feature uplifting stories where faith helps guide you through life's challenges and discover the promise of a new beginning.

FREE Value Over **$20**

YES! Please send me 2 FREE Love Inspired Romance novels and my 2 FREE mystery gifts (gifts are worth about $10 retail). After receiving them, if I don't wish to receive any more books, I can return the shipping statement marked "cancel." If I don't cancel, I will receive 6 brand-new novels every month and be billed just $5.24 each for the regular-print edition or $5.99 each for the larger-print edition in the U.S., or $5.74 each for the regular-print edition or $6.24 each for the larger-print edition in Canada. That's a savings of at least 13% off the cover price. It's quite a bargain! Shipping and handling is just 50¢ per book in the U.S. and $1.25 per book in Canada.* I understand that accepting the 2 free books and gifts places me under no obligation to buy anything. I can always return a shipment and cancel at any time. The free books and gifts are mine to keep no matter what I decide.

Choose one: ☐ **Love Inspired Romance**
     Regular-Print
     (105/305 IDN GNWC)

     ☐ **Love Inspired Romance**
     Larger-Print
     (122/322 IDN GNWC)

Name (please print)

Address   Apt. #

City   State/Province   Zip/Postal Code

Mail to the **Reader Service**:
IN U.S.A.: P.O. Box 1341, Buffalo, NY 14240-8531
IN CANADA: P.O. Box 603, Fort Erie, Ontario L2A 5X3

Want to try 2 free books from another series? Call 1-800-873-8635 or visit www.ReaderService.com.

---

*Terms and prices subject to change without notice. Prices do not include sales taxes, which will be charged (if applicable) based on your state or country of residence. Canadian residents will be charged applicable taxes. Offer not valid in Quebec. This offer is limited to one order per household. Books received may not be as shown. Not valid for current subscribers to Love Inspired Romance books. All orders subject to approval. Credit or debit balances in a customer's account(s) may be offset by any other outstanding balance owed by or to the customer. Please allow 4 to 6 weeks for delivery. Offer available while quantities last.

Your Privacy—The Reader Service is committed to protecting your privacy. Our Privacy Policy is available online at www.ReaderService.com or upon request from the Reader Service. We make a portion of our mailing list available to reputable third parties that offer products we believe may interest you. If you prefer that we not exchange your name with third parties, or if you wish to clarify or modify your communication preferences, please visit us at www.ReaderService.com/consumerschoice or write to us at Reader Service Preference Service, P.O. Box 9062, Buffalo, NY 14240-9062. Include your complete name and address.

LI20R

Get 4 **FREE REWARDS!**

We'll send you 2 FREE Books
<u>plus</u> 2 FREE Mystery Gifts.

Love Inspired Suspense
books showcase how
courage and optimism
unite in stories of faith and
love in the face of danger.

FREE
Value Over
$20

Get 4 FREE REWARDS!

We'll send you 2 FREE Books plus 2 FREE Mystery Gifts.

Harlequin Heartwarming Larger-Print books will connect you to uplifting stories where the bonds of friendship, family and community unite.

FREE Value Over $20

Get 4 FREE REWARDS!

We'll send you 2 FREE Books plus 2 FREE Mystery Gifts.

FREE
Value Over
$20

Both the **Romance** and **Suspense** collections feature compelling novels written by many of today's bestselling authors.

YES! Please send me 2 FREE novels from the Essential Romance or Essential Suspense Collection and my 2 FREE gifts (gifts are worth about $10 retail). After receiving them, if I don't wish to receive any more books, I can return the shipping statement marked "cancel." If I don't cancel, I will receive 4 brand-new novels every month and be billed just $6.99 each in the U.S. or $7.24 each in Canada. That's a savings of at least 13% off the cover price. It's quite a bargain! Shipping and handling is just 50¢ per book in the U.S. and $1.25 per book in Canada.* I understand that accepting the 2 free books and gifts places me under no obligation to buy anything. I can always return a shipment and cancel at any time. The free books and gifts are mine to keep no matter what I decide.

Choose one: ☐ **Essential Romance**
(194/394 MDN GNNP)

☐ **Essential Suspense**
(191/391 MDN GNNP)

Name (please print)

Address   Apt. #

City   State/Province   Zip/Postal Code

Mail to the **Reader Service:**
IN U.S.A.: P.O. Box 1341, Buffalo, NY 14240-8531
IN CANADA: P.O. Box 603, Fort Erie, Ontario L2A 5X3

Want to try 2 free books from another series? Call 1-800-873-8635 or visit www.ReaderService.com.

---

*Terms and prices subject to change without notice. Prices do not include sales taxes, which will be charged (if applicable) based on your state or country of residence. Canadian residents will be charged applicable taxes. Offer not valid in Quebec. This offer is limited to one order per household. Books received may not be as shown. Not valid for current subscribers to the Essential Romance or Essential Suspense Collection. All orders subject to approval. Credit or debit balances in a customer's account(s) may be offset by any other outstanding balance owed by or to the customer. Please allow 4 to 6 weeks for delivery. Offer available while quantities last.

Your Privacy—The Reader Service is committed to protecting your privacy. Our Privacy Policy is available online at www.ReaderService.com or upon request from the Reader Service. We make a portion of our mailing list available to reputable third parties that offer products we believe may interest you. If you prefer that we not exchange your name with third parties, or if you wish to clarify or modify your communication preferences, please visit us at www.ReaderService.com/consumerschoice or write to us at Reader Service Preference Service, P.O. Box 9062, Buffalo, NY 14240-9062. Include your complete name and address.

STRS20R

ReaderService.com has a new look!

We have refreshed our website and we want to share our new look with you. Head over to ReaderService.com and check it out!

On ReaderService.com, you can:

- Try 2 free books from any series
- Access risk-free special offers
- View your account history & manage payments
- Browse the latest Bonus Bucks catalog

Don't miss out!

If you want to stay up-to-date on the latest at the Reader Service and enjoy more Harlequin content, make sure you've signed up for our monthly News & Notes email newsletter. Sign up online at ReaderService.com.